E

Crowned copyright © Kristine Hauser, 2017
All rights reserved.

Spring Breeze Books

Cover art & design: Emma Van Dyke

For Mrs. Johnson, my seventh-grade English teacher. Wherever you are, and whatever you're doing now, I want you to know that I never would have made it this far without your encouragement of my wild thirteen-year-old imagination and your belief in magic

To the A-Kon convention and to the memories that were made there

To Stephanie, a breathless, brilliant editor. I owe you a bottle of the finest. Come collect anytime

For Bridget Blosser

To Liz, my own mysteriously encountered weirdo

To Mom and Michael, my first readers

For Phil, Zach, and Molly; as always

Table of Contents

The Queen of the Guardhouse	7
Glamor and Thread	51
Magnifikat	77
Ungodly Hour	123
Empty Spaces	133
Three Nerds and a Camera	165
To Hold	207

The Queen of the Guardhouse
K.R. Kampion

Ryaela Vaeliadatyr, the Crown Prince's bodyguard, halted at the entrance to the darkened hallway and held up a hand. Crown Prince Galeran Azaleesyn bumped into her shoulder. He started and fumbled the book he was carrying, not appearing to notice that several of the torches in the hallway were out.

"Ryaela." His voice was too loud. "What is it?"

Ryaela shushed him. "The torches, Galeran."

She strained her ears. The hall was quiet, save for the flutter of the remaining torch flames. Ryaela didn't like it. She'd seen these torches stay lit with entire squadrons rushing down the hallways. They didn't just burn out. Ryaela unslung her battleaxe from her back and held it ready. Her heart began a steady war drum pound in her chest. She took two steps in front of Galeran.

Metal hissed against leather as the Crown Prince unsheathed his pair of short swords. Ryaela heard his footsteps on the wood floor as he turned his back to Ryaela's to deter any surprise attacks.

"Will we proceed?" Galeran asked.

Ryaela listened for a few more seconds. Nothing but the whoosh of the torches and the hoot of an owl. She glared at the half-lit hallway.

"Yes," Ryaela replied. "Keep your position."

"Of course." She could hear the grin in Galeran's voice. "Eyes at your back."

As much as Ryaela hated admitting it, knowing Galeran was there calmed her. She smiled as she took one measured step into the hallway. Galeran's matching step echoed hers as he walked behind her, keeping the same amount of distance between them.

They made it halfway down the hallway when a sharp intake of breath hissed through the air. Before Ryaela could pinpoint where it came from, Galeran let out a shout.

"Look up!" he yelled.

A figure clad all in black dropped from the ceiling. A pair of fighting knives glinted in their hands. Ryaela snarled as her vision turned needle sharp on the intruder. Their face was covered, but their slender frame and long limbs betrayed elven heritage. Their black clothing was mottled with brown and dark green to match the palace's woodwork.

As soon as the intruder's feet touched the ground, Ryaela swung her axe. It swished over the intruder's head as they ducked low and tried to run at her. She halted them with a wicked kick, sending them staggering back.

Suddenly Galeran was on them, in a flurry of blades. The intruder lunged and caught one of Galeran's swords between their knife blades. With a flick of their wrists, they sent the sword spinning from his grasp. Galeran staggered back, fear flicking through his eyes.

Just as Ryaela hefted her axe to come to his aid, she caught a movement from just behind Galeran's shoulder.

"Galeran!" she shouted.

Galeran used his backwards momentum to drop to the ground and roll just as another intruder careened from the shadows. Ryaela snarled and swung at the intruder closest to Galeran. Of course, there were two of them!

The point of the axe took the first intruder in the shoulder, knocking them flat on their back. Blood soaked through their dark clothes. Ryaela whirled and went after the second intruder.

Galeran was still down, scrambling backwards as the second intruder bore down on him. He caught her eye before tucking and rolling to the side. The intruder turned just in time to take Ryaela's axe blade to the chest. Ryaela pulled her lips back from her teeth in a death's head grin as the intruder made a gurgling sound and went limp. She kicked the corpse to the ground.

"Ryaela!" Galeran shouted as he got to his feet.

Ryaela spun around, keeping Galeran in his place behind her, just in time to see the wounded assassin get up and go tearing down the hallway.

"Stay here!" Ryaela yelled over her shoulder as she took off after them. "Call reinforcements!"

"Yes, sir!" Galeran called back just before bellowing a call to arms.

Ryaela kept the living intruder in her sights as they rushed down the hallways, extinguishing torches with a soft word as they went. Godsdamned spellcasters!

Even with the cover of darkness, they were still wounded. The intruder wouldn't get far. If Ryaela caught them, she'd be promoted for sure. Few would-be royal assassins were ever taken alive: it would be a real feather in Ryaela's already laden cap. She would be a High General before the end of the week.

The intruder stumbled, and Ryaela picked up her pace. She was so close she could hear their ragged breathing.

Ryaela put on one final burst of speed and shot out a hand to grab the intruder. At the last second the intruder whirled and dashed something at Ryaela's feet. Thick, chalky smoke burst up from the ground and coated the inside of Ryaela's nose and mouth. She staggered, grit knifing through her lungs and began to cough.

No, no, godsdammit, no!

Ryaela stumbled backwards out of the smoke cloud and braced her hands on her knees. She cursed herself and that blasted assassin. Ryaela coughed some more and spat on the floor. Her saliva was brackish. She growled in disgust before coughing again.

Galeran. What if the assassin doubled back?

Fear knifed through her stomach. She had to get back to Galeran. Ryaela turned and rushed back, still coughing every other step. If something happened to him she would never forgive herself.

She turned the corner back into the hallway where she'd left Galeran. Half the palace guard had taken up positions at all the windows: she couldn't even see the Crown Prince.

"Captain!" Ryaela's second, Nila, disengaged herself from the cluster of guards in the middle of the hallway. In the decade Ryaela had known her, Nila had never succeeded at keeping her dark hair in the warriors' braid. It was constantly slipping loose and frizzing about her face like a mane. "What happened to you?"

"Bastard threw a chalk bomb," Ryaela muttered, cheeks heating with anger. Nila was never going to let her live this down. "They didn't double back, did they?"

"We haven't seen anything," Nila replied. "His Majesty almost brought the place down with his shouting. I'm surprised he didn't rouse the king and queen."

"I'm surprised the bastard didn't come back to silence him," Ryaela said.

Nila snorted a laugh, "Too bad you didn't get him."

"Don't remind me," Ryaela rolled her eyes. There went that early promotion.

"I guess the only good news is The Bastard will probably be back," Nila said with a glance at the windows.

Ryaela gripped her axe. That was true. She didn't want to be excited about someone trying to kill Galeran, but the thought of being able to take that clever bastard down made her blood sing.

"Ryaela!"

Galeran muscled his way out of the circle of guards, book still tucked into his sword belt. Ryaela stood up straighter and bowed slightly before meeting his eyes.

"Are you all right?" Galeran asked. "What happened to the assassin?"

"I'm fine, Your Majesty," Ryaela replied. "The assassin escaped; threw a chalk bomb in the adjacent hallway and then ran like a coward."

"Typical," Galeran snorted.

"Has anyone taken a look at the body?" Ryaela asked, casting a glance at the second assassin's corpse.

"Not yet," Galeran said. "I had them hold off and wait for you."

Ryaela gave him a grateful smile before turning her attention to the corpse. "Shall we see what we've got, Your Majesty?"

"Of course," Galeran smiled back before crouching beside the body.

Ryaela waved Nila over. Between the three of them, Ryaela knew they'd be able to glean something.

The corpse lay on its back in a pool of its own blood, arms outstretched, still clutching its pair of fighting daggers. Nila immediately pried one of the blades free and held it up to scrutinize it.

"Ghost dagger," she muttered, running a thumb over the strange runes etched into the almost black blade. "Definitely professionals. Based on the curve of the blade, I'd say these two were made by the mountain elves."

"Of course," Ryaela muttered. There was only one type of adversary that Ryaela had ever seen wield the infamous returning blades. They required a very specific type of enchantment not often practiced in the light of day.

Galeran, meanwhile, tugged the assassin's face covering free, revealing a handsome elven face. He wasn't old, perhaps 200 years. His skin held the grayish tint typical of the mountain elves, made grayer in death. Galeran exchanged a glance with Ryaela.

The mountain elf kingdom of Stratisfae had been launching border skirmishes against the Oranteon elves for centuries. They envied the power the ageless forest held within its roots and branches. The dead rocks of the Gartheon Mountains did not fuel magic the way a living forest, especially one as ancient as Oranteon, could. The elves of Stratisfae fancied themselves true masters of magic, and felt entitled to the forest and its power. But Oranteon never chose them. And the elves of Stratisfae had never made it to Oranteon's heart. Not until now.

"Lift him up," Ryaela ordered, briefly forgetting Galeran's title. "Your Majesty."

Nila raised an eyebrow. Galeran cracked a smirk, before lifting the corpse up by the shoulders. Ryaela went to work opening the assassin's black tunic enough to expose the skin of his right shoulder.

A small tattoo of a white square in the center of a black circle greeted her eyes. The Black Guild. How on earth had he gotten in? No assassin from Stratisfae had ever made it into the capital city.

"How is this possible?" Galeran voiced her thoughts.

"Doesn't Spymaster Elsharra have an informant in the Black Guild?" Nila asked.

"I believe so," Ryaela replied, looking hard at the assassin's face. "She probably knows something. Nila, have someone move the body. I will escort His Majesty back to his chambers."

"Yes, sir," Nila saluted and immediately began barking orders at the other guards.

"Come, sire," Ryaela stood up. "Let's get you to safety."

"I'm safe right now." Galeran gave her a crooked grin that should not have made her chest feel so warm.

Ryaela smiled back and led him down the main hall towards his rooms. Galeran walked at her side, one hand on the short sword at his hip.

"Are you certain you're all right, Galeran?" Ryaela asked him once they were out of everyone else's earshot. Once she became his personal guard, Galeran told her that if she was going to be stuck watching him sleep and prancing around his chambers half-naked, they had to be on a first-name basis. That memory still made her smile.

"I'm fine, Ryaela," Galeran replied. "Have I ever lied about that?"

"Yes, actually, you have. You rode home with two broken ribs and your mother almost beheaded me," Ryaela said.

Galeran looked sheepish. "I'd hoped you were too injured to remember that."

"Please, Galeran. You know I remember everything," Ryaela grinned at him.

"Fair enough, my lady," Galeran laughed.

Ryaela felt a little heat rise to her face. Galeran had recently taken to calling her that when they were alone. She wasn't sure what it was about the way he said it that she liked so much. Perhaps it was something in his smile.

"Damn," Galeran said suddenly.

"What?" Ryaela asked. She scanned the hallway, half-expecting him to have seen something.

"I should've asked Nila if I could have the dead one's ghost daggers," Galeran said.

"Seriously, Galeran?" Ryaela asked. "You want to touch those things? You know they only work for their chosen wielder."

"They can change wielders, I've read about how it's done," Galeran said. "Come on, you know I need all the help I can get. It's totally worth the chance they'll reject."

The twinkle in his eye told her he was joking but Ryaela pursed her lips anyway. "If you want to try having your soul bound to a pair of shitty daggers wielded by someone who tried to murder you, be my guest."

"I suppose you make a good point," Galeran sighed.

15

Ryaela rolled her eyes and rubbed her thumb over the handle of her trusty axe. It was the chosen weapon of the Oranteon military since its formation. Both a tool of destruction and rebuilding, it was a versatile weapon for those who called Oranteon home. Although they never touched the living trees.

They arrived at Galeran's chambers and Ryaela entered first, just in case The Bastard had found their way there after throwing the chalk bomb. She took a few steps into his bedroom and listened, keeping a tight grip on her axe. The room was quiet, but not disturbingly so. Trees whispered through the windows, and another owl hooted. The adrenaline in her veins abated. Ryaela turned back to Galeran and nodded once, lowering her axe. Galeran smiled and returned the nod before striding into the room and lighting the nearest lamp.

"Feel free to use the washroom," he said as he removed the belt with his short swords. "You have chalk dust in your hair. White really isn't your color, I much prefer the blond."

Ryaela stuck her tongue out at him as she headed in the direction of the washroom. The chalk made her scalp and neck itch.

After she'd washed her face and hair the best she could, Ryaela returned to Galeran's bedroom. He was still awake and reading yet another book by the lamplight with the blankets half off him. Galeran never wore a shirt to sleep and Ryaela flicked her eyes down his lean torso as she moved to her customary night post.

Galeran looked up from his book and smiled at her before setting the book aside. "I suppose I'll be going to sleep now so you can have a blissful few hours free of me."

"If only," Ryaela rolled her eyes.

Galeran laughed and pulled up the blankets as he lay down. "Be careful what you wish for, there are assassins about."

"Don't remind me," Ryaela huffed. "Bastards."

Galeran laughed again and settled under his blankets before turning out the lamp. The room went dark and it took Ryaela's eyes a split second to adjust to the gloom. She could hear Galeran trying to get comfortable. Ryaela sat in her chair by the window and closed her eyes.

"Good night, Ryaela," Galeran said softly. "And thank you, for saving my life."

"Good night," Ryaela replied. "And you don't have to thank me every time I save your sorry ass. It's kind of my job."

"Don't tell me what to do," Galeran's voice was tired, but she could still hear laughter there. "I'm the crown prince."

"And *I* heard you mutter 'tits' in your sleep last night."

"I relent, my lady."

"I thought you might," Ryaela chuckled.

"I'm going to sleep now, I swear," Galeran said. "Good night."

"Good night." Ryaela hesitated a moment. She never said Galeran's name when she bid him good night. It felt too intimate. But tonight wasn't the first night she wanted to.

17

*   *   *

The next morning found Ryaela and Galeran making their way to the throne room. They wove around the massive tree trunks that held up the ceilings. The palace was built over the heart of Oranteon. Its largest trees made the palace's foundation and braced its vaulting rooftop. Oranteon supported them, while the elves protected its heart. Sometimes Ryaela thought she could feel it beat beneath her feet.

Ryaela watched the ceilings and the shadows for any would-be assassins. She was not about to get dropped on a second time.

"I'm quite certain you'd be able to freeze any attackers in place with that snarl, my lady," Galeran hadn't slept well. Ryaela could tell.

"Good," Ryaela replied. "Makes it easier to kill them that way."

Galeran laughed out loud as they entered the throne room shoulder to shoulder. Ryaela smiled just a little.

The throne room was the largest room in the palace. A massive tree stood proudly in the center of the circular room, holding the roof in its lower branches.

Queen Azalee and King Veldar were already seated on their twin thrones, nestled in the great tree's roots. They both looked imposing even in their plain clothing. Queen Azalee's pale blue dress covered her feet in a shimmering pool and her black hair was loose about her shoulders. King Veldar sat tall in a sleeveless tunic with winged shoulders. His hair fell down his back in the customary single braid of a warrior.

To the queen's left sat the two less ornate thrones reserved for the Crown Princes. Dalziel, Galeran's younger brother, already slouched in his seat, warhammer resting against its side. He was more muscular than Galeran, with massive shoulders. The tight warrior's braid he wore drew attention to the fact that one of his pointed ears had an obvious nick in it. He wore his scars proudly, looking every inch the warrior of Oranteon. But his eyes lacked Galeran's clever spark.

Dalziel's bodyguard, Serae, stood just behind the throne. She was the shortest member of the palace guards but she more than made up for it in strength. The axe she carried should have been too big for her but Ryaela had seen her wield it like it weighed nothing. She caught Ryaela's eye and smiled.

Dalziel sneered as Galeran ascended the steps to his throne. "I must congratulate you; three whole seconds before hiding behind your bodyguard, I think that's a new record."

Galeran's face twitched as he sat down. Queen Azalee turned sharply and glared at her younger son but King Veldar chuckled softly. Ryaela swallowed the urge to retort. Dalziel was not her concern.

The doors to the throne room opened again. Nila strode in shoulder to shoulder with Elsharra Haldriethdatyr, the royal spymaster. Elsharra looked as composed as ever. Her auburn hair, a collection of tiny braids, was gathered in a bunch at the nape of her neck. Not a single one was out of place. Nila shot her an envious look before they both bowed to the royal family.

"Please make your report," Queen Azalee ordered.

Ryaela and Nila gave their accounts of the assassination attempt with occasional elaboration from Galeran.

Dalziel's eyes narrowed as they spoke of the Black Guild assassin and the survivor. The queen and king looked disturbed.

"Do you have any idea where the survivor could be?" Queen Azalee's voice was terse.

"Close by," Ryaela replied. "They made it this far. I can't imagine they would forfeit the chance to strike again. Injured or not."

"Elsharra, have you noticed any changes in behavior among the servants?" Galeran spoke up. "Since this assassin is a spellcaster, they might be able to disguise themselves. There are spells for that, right?"

"Yes, sire," Elsharra nodded. "I haven't noticed anything, but I will begin screening the servants immediately if you so desire."

"I do," Galeran said. "Thank you."

"Excellent idea, Galeran," Queen Azalee gave a proud smile. Dalziel rolled his eyes.

"The fact that they've chosen to target Galeran is disturbing," King Veldar leaned back in his throne and pressed his knuckles to his lips.

"Indeed it is, but a very effective tactic, unfortunately," Queen Azalee sighed. "You remember what happened in the troll kingdom when Old King Tzuljin's first daughter was killed?"

"Can you please not talk about this assassination attempt like it already killed me, Mother?" Galeran asked.

"Come now, we're just preparing for the inevitable," Dalziel said. "Don't deny us that."

"Inevitable," Galeran's voice was like ice. "Care to elaborate on that, Dalziel?"

"What?" Dalziel asked. "Oh, come on! It was a joke! I'm trying to make light of the situation for heaven's sake! But if you *want* to take it literally—"

"Boys!" Queen Azalee snapped. Her voice echoed through the throne room. "Enough! We already have one assassin loose in the city, I don't need you two at each other's throats!"

Ryaela let go of her axe as Dalziel and Galeran glowered at each other but leaned back in their thrones. Nila let out a breath, blowing a loose strand of hair off her forehead.

"Do you have any idea how a mountain elf from the Black Guild managed to get here, Spymaster Haldriethdatyr?" Queen Azalee addressed Elsharra.

"As of now, very little," Elsharra said. "But I do have several theories. One of them being this is the smallest incursion we've seen thus far. There were only two assassins. Even if Oranteon could make their travel inconvenient, smaller forces are much more difficult to halt."

"Could I propose a theory?" Galeran asked.

"Please do, Your Majesty," Elsharra replied.

"Perhaps invasion was not their goal," Galeran said slowly.

"What do you mean?" Ryaela spoke up. Nila elbowed her in the ribs and Ryaela added, "Your Majesty?"

"Perhaps they have a different set of goals that have nothing to do with Oranteon," Galeran continued. "Perhaps we're dealing with something else entirely."

"Ga—Your Majesty," Ryaela said. "Someone tried to assassinate you. If this doesn't have to do with Oranteon, what reason could they have?"

You spend half your time in the library, the other quarter training, and the other quarter being too good-natured for your own good, Ryaela wanted to say.

Galeran shrugged, "I'm the Crown Prince. I must have done something that pissed someone in Oranteon off. Try as I might, not everyone is happy I'm going to be the next king."

Dalziel's face went livid. He may not have been clever, but Galeran's tone left little to the imagination. The throne room went silent as an abandoned battlefield.

"Oh gods be damned," Nila muttered.

"Care to elaborate on that, my dear brother?" Dalziel's voice was dangerous.

Ryaela gripped the handle of her axe again. Galeran wouldn't last a minute against his brother if it came to blows.

"I don't know, do you think it's necessary?" Galeran replied, face hard as steel.

"Dalziel! Galeran!" Queen Azalee snapped. "For the love of the gods, stop it!"

"I've had enough of this!" Dalziel spat as he rose from his throne. "Think what you want! See what good it'll do you when they strike again!"

"Dalziel!" Queen Azalee called after him as he stalked past Ryaela towards the doors.

Serae shot Ryaela an apologetic glance as she followed Dalziel from the throne room. The door shut behind them with a sound like thunder. Ryaela let go of her axe and turned her attention back to the remaining royal family. Galeran glared at the throne room doors with his fists clenched. Queen Azalee put her face in her hands while King Veldar rubbed her back. Silence reigned for several unbearable moments before Elsharra softly cleared her throat.

"I know no one wants to hear it," she began. "But I think we should take Prince Galeran's theory into consideration."

"My son is *not* a traitor!" King Veldar snapped, fixing Elsharra in a venomous glare.

"I didn't say that," Elsharra said. "But I don't think we should rule out the idea of a traitor within Oranteon. It's quite likely that someone of very high status granted the assassins passage through to the capital city, and then into the palace."

Ryaela and Nila exchanged a glance. Dalziel wasn't clever, but he was vicious. Ryaela never thought he would go as far as to try to have his brother killed. But she knew Galeran was afraid of him, and that was enough reason for Ryaela to be wary.

"So what do you propose we do?" Queen Azalee asked.

"Are you going to interrogate my son?"

"Hopefully it won't come to that," Elsharra said. "But I would like to have someone watch him."

"His bodyguard, Serae, is part of my squadron," Ryaela spoke up. "If he's planning anything, she would know. Nila and I could speak to her, if you like." Nila shot her another reproachful glance. "Your Majesty."

"Please do," Queen Azalee nodded. "Also screen the servants, be watchful for any odd behavior. As of this moment, I want the palace locked down. No one is allowed in or out until this assassin is caught. Is that clear?"

"Yes, Your Majesty." Ryaela, Nila, and Elsharra chorused.

"Captain Vaeliadatyr, I want you in charge of the investigation," Queen Azalee continued.

Ryaela's heart leapt. Had she just been promoted? She shot an excited grin at Nila before turning back to the queen.

"Spymaster Haldriethdatyr," Queen Azalee went on. "I want you to report your findings to Captain Vaeliadatyr first and foremost."

"Yes, Your Majesty," Elsharra said with a small bow.

"That is all," Queen Azalee said. "I expect reports from you at the end of each day, Captain."

"Of course, Your Majesty," Ryaela bowed. "What of my other duties?"

"If I may interject, Mother," Galeran spoke up. "Despite the investigation, I'm quite certain I'll be safer at the Captain's side. Only if it's all right with you, Captain Vaeliadatyr."

Ryaela weighed her options. Galeran wasn't the best fighter, but he was extremely smart and the assassin's primary target. His presence in the investigation might draw The Bastard out. Ryaela nodded once and smiled. "Yes, Your Majesty. Your presence would be welcome."

Galeran grinned at her. Ryaela caught Nila rolling her eyes.

"Then it's settled," Queen Azalee said. "All of you are dismissed. You as well, Galeran."

Elsharra bowed and left the room without another word. Once Galeran alighted from the dais, Ryaela and Nila left the throne room. Elsharra was waiting for them outside the doors.

"Congratulations on the promotion, Captain Vaeliadatyr," she said with a smile. "I must say, I expected no less from the Queen the of Guardhouse."

"Shut up, Elsharra, you know I hate that title," Ryaela rolled her eyes. She may have been the captain of the palace guards but she still had to answer to Queen Azalee's guard, Lieutenant Marqwynsyn. She wasn't entirely sure when the nickname first started. But it was probably around the time she took command of

25

Captain Marqwynsyn's entire squadron when he'd fallen in an ogre attack.

"Still," Elsharra shrugged. "Just take the compliment, it's well deserved."

"Thanks, Elsharra," Ryaela smiled before turning to her second. "Nila, go to the guardhouse and tell the rest of the squadron we're in lockdown. Ensure they act accordingly."

"Yes, sir," Nila said. "When do you want to talk to Serae?"

"When she gets off duty," Ryaela replied. "We don't want Prince Dalziel to suspect he's under surveillance."

"Of course," Nila nodded. "What are you going to do?"

"I'm going to continue business as usual for now and see if The Bastard shows their face again," Ryaela said.

"I would like to go with Spymaster Haldriethdatyr," Galeran added with a nod towards Elsharra. "If it's all right with you, I would like to know what you're asking the servants. That alone might give us a lead."

"Of course, Your Majesty," Elsharra bowed. "I would very much appreciate your keen eyes and second opinion."

"I am at your disposal," Galeran return the bow with a grin.

"Fair enough," Nila answered. "I will take my leave, Captain, Your Majesty."

Ryaela saluted and Galeran nodded as Nila marched off down the hallway.

"Why do I feel like all this is a waste of time?" Nila complained as she and Ryaela put on their armor in the palace guardhouse. The guardhouse had been Ryaela's home for the past five years. It was a glorified barracks attached to the palace by a covered walkway through the gardens. However, instead of hard cots, the palace guards enjoyed the luxury of actual beds. The quarters were a bit cramped, but there were no complaints from Ryaela.

"I don't think it has been," Ryaela said. It had been a week since the assassin struck. She and Nila had interviewed Serae several times but discovered nothing. Dalziel frequently voiced his dislike of his older brother but never expressed a desire to see him die. After the upset in the throne room, Dalziel had gone straight to the training field to pour his rage into a furious series of hammer blows meant for the assassin's head. Apparently, he wanted to beat them to a bloody mash for sullying his reputation. Before that, his time was spaced equally between training, hunting monsters with the border patrol, and making weapons in the royal forge. After, he had even gone as far as to offer to help hunt the assassin down.

"I just don't think Prince Dalziel is our traitor," she went on. "I'd trust Serae with my life. She's one of us. I know she never lets Dalziel out of her sight and he likes her too damn much to keep something like that from her."

"I guess," Nila tried and failed to wrangle a strand of hair back into her warriors' braid. "But if Elsharra doesn't uncover anything from the servants, he's still our most likely suspect."

"I know," Ryaela sighed. "Galeran suspects him even after he offered to help. But I don't blame him. Dalziel has done nothing but bully him ever since they were little."

"I always thought bullying was the older sibling's job," Nila gave Ryaela a playful nudge.

"Shut up, Nila! I never bullied my little brothers!" Ryaela shoved her back.

"That's not what they tell me," Nila replied.

"Well, they're liars!" Ryaela raised herself up to her full height, standing several inches taller than Nila.

Nila laughed, "Keep telling yourself that."

"How dare you!" Ryaela gave Nila one last playful shove as they left the guardhouse. Ryaela needed to return to guarding Galeran for the night while Nila patrolled the palace halls.

The number of palace guards patrolling the hallways had doubled since the attack. Their murmuring voices echoed against the palace's vaulted ceilings. The guards snapped to attention as Ryaela strode by. She gave them an approving nod.

They arrived at Galeran's room and the two extra guards stationed there immediately moved aside to grant them entry. Ryaela could hear voices inside. She didn't remember Galeran having any audiences that night. A spike of apprehension pierced her chest. Ryaela opened the door quickly to find Galeran and Elsharra deeply engaged in conversation.

"Captain Vaeliadatyr," Elsharra's face brightened as Ryaela approached. "Sergeant Brynoredatyr. I was just about to have someone fetch you both. I've just acquired some new evidence in the case."

"Why didn't you tell me immediately?" Ryaela asked, narrowing her eyes. "The queen ordered that you report all of your findings to me first."

She flicked her eyes towards Galeran. His handsome face was tight with worry and anger. He didn't seem to notice she was there. Ryaela's chest went cold as she turned back to Elsharra for an explanation.

"Forgive me, Captain," Elsharra said. "But the information is of an extremely sensitive nature, and I thought it was only right for His Majesty to learn of it first."

"What is this evidence?" Ryaela demanded. "What have you found?"

"One of the servants reported Prince Dalziel sneaking out of the palace after midnight about three days before the attempt on Galeran's life," Elsharra said.

"What?" Ryaela asked. "Who? Who made the report?"

"One of the steward's assistants," Elsharra said. "She was coming back from a tryst with one of the stable hands when she saw him sneaking through the gardens."

"Is she certain it was Prince Dalziel?" Ryaela asked. This didn't match any of Serae's statements. Could she have lied to protect Dalziel?

"She swears on her life," Elsharra replied.

"Why didn't she speak up at the beginning of the inquiries?" Ryaela asked.

"She was afraid of speaking up about the tryst," Elsharra shook her head. "Apparently, she'd been forbidden from seeing him."

Nila crossed her arms and looked to Ryaela for guidance. Ryaela took a deep breath and let it out slowly. This was the best lead they'd gotten so far, but something about it just didn't feel right. Ryaela trusted Serae. She had trained with her when she first became Galeran's bodyguard. If Dalziel were committing treason, Serae would have acted regardless of how she felt about him. Wouldn't she?

Nila let out a low whistle, "That's...quite an accusation, Spymaster Haldriethdatyr. What do you make of this, Your Majesty?"

"I don't know." Galeran's voice was small. He was so afraid. Ryaela wanted to punch all his fears in the face. "We need more evidence. It doesn't match several other statements that we've already acquired. We need to figure out who the liars are. Now, I'm very tired. Spymaster Haldriethdatyr, Sergeant Brynoredatyr, you're both dismissed."

Elsharra and Nila bowed low before leaving the room and closing the door. Galeran stood up slowly, tension radiating from him, and began to pace.

"Galeran," Ryaela said softly.

Galeran stopped pacing and took a deep breath, "Ryaela, please, take me outside."

"Galeran." The palace was in lockdown. She couldn't risk delivering him to any assassins waiting outside.

"I can't be in here anymore!" Galeran burst out. "This place is stifling! Please, for the love of the gods, Ryaela, just let me into Oranteon. Just for a moment."

Ryaela's chest felt tight. She hated seeing him like this. She missed his laugh, his crooked smile. If The Bastard showed their cloaked face out there, she was going to tear it off.

"We'll have to hurry before anyone notices we're out there," Ryaela said. "I may be Queen of the Guardhouse, but your mother will probably demand an explanation."

"Of course, Ryaela," Galeran gave her a shadow of his usual grin. "Thank you."

"Don't thank me before we're out there," Ryaela smiled back. "Come on."

It took both Ryaela and Galeran pulling rank on the guards at the door to get them to let the two of them out of the palace. Once outside, Ryaela closed her eyes and took a deep breath. Oranteon smelled of an early fall; of damp earth and drying leaves. The forest sighed and a soft breeze caressed her cheeks and neck. She smiled and glanced at Galeran.

His eyes were still closed and some of the tension eased from his face. Oranteon whispered, and Ryaela felt the breeze warm slightly as it played with a loose strand of her hair.

Oranteon was ancient when Ryaela's people first settled there so many millennia ago. The tree trunks around them were wide enough for Ryaela and Galeran to lean against them shoulder to shoulder. It was ageless and fathomless in its knowledge. The air pulsed with life and magic. Oranteon *knew* they were there.

Galeran stopped walking and looked up at the sky for a few moments before speaking, "I don't know what to think, Ryaela."

"About what?" Ryaela asked, taking a small step towards him.

"About this entire investigation," Galeran said. "About my brother." He crossed his arms and gripped his biceps.

"Do you think he's the traitor?" Ryaela asked. If Dalziel truly were the traitor, Ryaela would kill him with her bare hands. Oranteon hissed and the breeze grew colder. This forest was her home, and she would not allow anyone to take it from her.

Galeran shook his head, "I don't know. Dalziel and I have never been...Ryaela, I don't want to be the king that executes his own brother. I never wanted that. I never wanted to...drive him to this." He lowered his eyes and stared at the ground, jaw working. "The statements don't match; Serae's and Elsharra's. Someone is lying and I can't—"

"Galeran," Ryaela cut him off as she went to him and rested her hands against his upper arms. He wouldn't think clearly if he was so afraid. His skin was chilly and covered in gooseflesh. She wanted to warm him just a little. "The investigation is still in its early stages. We don't have enough information to know if Dalziel is the traitor or not. We have one account of him sneaking out, and several solid alibis." Ryaela gently rubbed his arms. "We need to talk to the steward's assistant and verify it before telling anyone else."

"Do you think Dalziel is a traitor, Ryaela?" Galeran asked.

"Because right now, he's the only one that makes sense. But this doesn't feel like something he would do. We've never been close, but I know him well enough to know he's never had the patience for subterfuge. I always figured that if he were going to challenge me, he would just do it. He knows I wouldn't last ten minutes against him in combat." Galeran let out a panicked laugh and shook his head.

"To be completely honest, Galeran," Ryaela replied, "I don't think your brother is the traitor. His bodyguard, Serae, she and I trained together. She's not the kind of person who would just let Dalziel commit treason, regardless of how she felt about him. I don't think she would lie for him." Ryaela paused and another idea came to her. "Besides, you said so yourself, this assassin might be able to disguise themselves. What's to stop them from disguising themselves as your brother?"

Galeran stared at her for a moment, a spark of hope flaring in his dark eyes. "That is very true, my lady."

"Trust your instincts." Ryaela moved one hand from his arm to rest against his chest, over his heart. "You know I do."

Ryaela realized that she might have gone too far. She had never touched him like this before, but she didn't want to move away. Galeran's breathing quickened as he looked back at her, chest rising and falling under her hand. Ryaela gave him a small, fierce smile.

"And I trust yours, my lady." Galeran flashed his crooked grin and covered her hand with his. It was cool and rough with calluses. "I think I trust yours more than anyone else's. I always have."

"Then you will remember I fight for Oranteon," Ryaela replied. *And for you.* "If the worst happens, and your brother is one of its enemies then I will kill him. And it will not be your fault. But for now, we need to focus on figuring out what's truly going on here. Because you're right, something doesn't add up."

Galeran closed his eyes briefly and nodded. Oranteon whispered around them as if agreeing. When Galeran opened his eyes again, he took her hand and raised it to his lips. Ryaela couldn't keep her breath from catching as his lips brushed over her skin like a moth's wings.

"We should go back inside." Galeran lowered her hand and stepped back. "I'm going to need to sleep if my instincts are going to be of any use."

Ryaela nodded and felt heat on her cheeks as Galeran turned to head back to the palace. The breeze from Oranteon suddenly blew colder and Ryaela tensed. She couldn't shake the feeling that someone had seen them.

*   *   *

Ryaela left Galeran's side the next morning to find Nila and interview the steward's assistant. She had extra guards stationed at his door, and hoped that would be enough. Her steps sounded supernaturally loud as she walked down the hallway towards the guardhouse. Ryaela kept an iron grip on her axe and bared her teeth at the shadows.

Four guards stood at intervals down the corridor towards the guardhouse. They all looked asleep.

"Look alive," Ryaela barked.

One of them slid to the floor, armor clattering against the stones. The wall behind him was splattered with blood. Ryaela let out a shout just as a small sound came from behind. One of the guards behind her lunged, armor melting away to be replaced by plain black clothing. A pair of black ghost daggers flashed towards her. The same mocking eyes gleamed at her over a black face covering.

"To me! To me!" Ryaela roared. "Breach! Breach!"

The assassin ducked low beneath her axe and slashed at her unarmored legs. Ryaela spun away and kicked out, swinging her axe as the assassin backpedaled. The blade whiffed over their head. If she could keep them here, it would buy enough time for backup to arrive.

The assassin snapped their fingers, sending a bolt of white energy at her. It took Ryaela high in the chest, slamming her into the wall. She cracked her head against the wood and saw spots. Ryaela gritted her teeth before pushing off the wall. Adrenaline shot through her veins like molten iron.

The Bastard waited a split second before slipping to the side. Ryaela tried to follow them with her axe but The Bastard was too quick. She buried her axe in the floor only inches from where the assassin had been. The shock of hitting the hardwood floor shuddered up Ryaela's arms. The Bastard kicked up, catching her in the jaw.

Ryaela grunted as the kick snapped her head back. She tasted iron in the back of her throat. Ryaela avoided The Bastard's next blow and snatched her emergency dagger from the sheath at her thigh. She sliced into their arm as they passed her again and felt a cold satisfaction as she cut flesh.

The Bastard hissed and lunged for her, slashing at her shoulder and neck. Ryaela felt the steel bite her shoulder, but barely registered the pain. She backpedaled as the second knife swished past her throat. Ryaela's axe was still stuck in the floor a few feet away. When she tried to move towards it, the assassin appeared in front of her, slashing at her face. Ryaela snarled and shifted into a low stance. She blocked The Bastard's knife with her forearm and stabbed at their stomach.

Searing pain ripped through Ryaela's senses and she let out a cry. The assassin rammed their second knife deep into her thigh. Her leg buckled and she went down on one knee. Godsdamn that Bastard! She'd let them get too close. The assassin chuckled and lunged again with their second knife.

"No you don't!" Ryaela snarled as her vision went red. She was not going to die at the hands of this smug bastard who didn't even have the courage to show their face.

She pushed off with her uninjured leg and slammed into the assassin's legs, knocking them flat on their back. Ryaela heard the air whoosh from their lungs and she grinned. She grappled them, holding her dagger at their throat. For the first time, the eyes were afraid. Ryaela bared her teeth and pressed the dagger hard into their flesh.

"Who hired you?" she demanded.

"Go to hell," The Bastard hissed.

Another blast of searing pain burst across Ryaela's back. She saw lights and a scream tore from her throat. The second dagger.

The assassin kicked her away and she landed hard, driving the dagger in deeper. Ryaela bit back another scream as the steel bit through her muscle. She could still breathe. The dagger hadn't punctured her lung. Ryaela tried to get up but couldn't force her body to cooperate. It felt like she was slowly turning into wood.

Suddenly the cold steel was ripped from her back and leg and hot blood gushed from the wounds. Godsdamned ghost daggers! Ryaela let out an enraged roar at the assassin as they calmly stood up. "Come at me, Bastard!"

"Ryaela! Breach! Sound the alarm! Breach!"

The edges of her vision blackened like the corners of a burning page. The Bastard crouched like a startled cat as someone leapt over Ryaela, blocking her from the assassin. An axe blade gleamed in her hands. Nila.

Nila swung her axe in an arc, driving the assassin back. *Idiot! Don't chase them off! Take them alive! Take them alive dammit!*

The Bastard feinted at Nila and tried to slip around her. Suddenly Galeran appeared, brandishing his short swords. He barred the assassin's way. The assassin backed up again before turning tail and nearly running into yet another guard with an axe.

"Don't let them run!" Ryaela yelled from the ground. Her back burned its protest at her shouting. "Drag that bastard back to me!"

"Chase them down!" Nila's voice shouted. It sounded farther away than it should have. The blackened edges of Ryaela's vision began to seep towards the center. She growled and tried to force them back.

"Ryaela! Ryaela," Suddenly, Galeran was at her side. He caressed the side of her face, tilting it up to look at him. His black eyes gleamed almost feverishly in her darkening vision and his handsome face was taut with worry. "Come on, let's get you to a healer. Come on."

He wrapped his arm around her waist and half dragged, half carried her to her feet. She draped her arm around his shoulders and snarled in pain as her injured leg briefly bore some weight. The black edges of her vision briefly receded, but she leaned heavily on Galeran as he helped her from the corridor.

* * *

A dull ache in her back and thigh roused Ryaela from sleep. She groggily opened her eyes to find herself in the healer's quarters. The room was small, a fireplace across from the bed, and a window beside it. It was nearly dusk outside.

The assassin! A jolt of panic shot through Ryaela's chest and she tried to sit up.

"Easy. Just because Healer Uriyah is the best palace healer we've had so far doesn't mean you can go running off just yet."

Ryaela turned to see Galeran seated in a comfortable chair at her bedside. His swords lay across his lap. As always, there was a book in his hand. His shoulders were pulled taut and his eyes constantly darted towards the sole window.

"I'm assuming The Bastard eluded us again," Ryaela said with a sigh.

Galeran nodded once with a rueful smile, "How'd you guess?"

Ryaela snorted, "You're going to need a better chess face if you want to hide anything from me. Where are Nila and Elsharra?"

"Nila is questioning the steward's assistant, and Elsharra is berating her underlings for letting this assassin slip under their noses again," Galeran said. "But we do know one thing, I'm not the target. Dalziel isn't the culprit."

"What?" Ryaela asked. "Why would they attack me if not to get to you?"

"Come on, Ryaela," Galeran gave her a long-suffering look. "Look at the facts here. They can disguise themselves to look like anyone, my brother included. They went out of their way to kill you in a head-on duel. Not stabbing you in the back when you weren't looking. Not sending another assassin to take me out while you were distracted. This assassin is after you and you alone. I'm an afterthought here. They want you dead and they nearly succeeded."

Ryaela felt her stomach drop. An assassin after her? Sure, she was the crown prince's bodyguard and the many times she'd saved his life probably didn't make her any friends among the mountain elves. Or anyone else that hated the Oranteon royal family. But she'd always assumed if there was a price on her head, it was because of her associations.

"After me?" Ryaela asked. "As vital as I am to keeping you alive, I don't see what can be accomplished solely by eliminating me."

Galeran stared at her for a few seconds with a look that was one part disbelief and another part something Ryaela wasn't sure she could place.

"My lady, I thought you of all people wouldn't need to be told how necessary you are to Oranteon. And to me."

Ryaela stared back and felt her heart speed up. He was right. If she fell, she couldn't imagine what would happen to Galeran, or to the rest of her guards. If The Bastard thought they could eliminate her, they had another thing coming.

Galeran sat across from her, nervousness making him look peaky. She knew he was afraid he'd overstepped. Ryaela tentatively reached a hand towards him. Galeran sat for a moment before rising from his chair to kneel at her bedside and take her hand. It was warm and his grip was firm. Ryaela flushed. She'd always liked his hands.

"We need a plan of action," Ryaela said. "Since I assumed the assassin was targeting you, we've been looking at all the wrong people."

"That's true, my lady," Galeran said.

"We're definitely still dealing with a traitor," Ryaela went on. "That's the only explanation for how they've been able to keep getting in."

"I agree," Galeran gripped her hand a little tighter. "And they want to frame my brother for treason. Can you think of anyone you've had any disputes with recently? Anyone that might be holding a grudge. I can think of several on my brother's end, but not as many on yours."

Ryaela ran through the names of her troops and she couldn't think of any that would dream of wanting her dead. She shook her head.

"There might be a few council members that think you hold too much sway over my family and me and see Dalziel as a nuisance," Galeran said. "I know Councilman Ydris isn't fond of either of you."

"Councilman Ydris isn't fond of anyone who disagrees with him too loudly," Ryaela replied. "But from what I know, he's all bluster. I'll ask Elsharra to keep her ears open."

Galeran thought for a moment and glanced at their entwined hands. He was planning something, she could see it in the set of his mouth. "How many people do you trust in the palace?"

Ryaela raised an eyebrow as she counted them. "You, of course, the king and queen, Nila, the rest of my troop. Why? Do you have an idea of who's behind this?"

"No," Galeran shook his head. "I just don't want anyone you don't absolutely trust involved. Elsharra has ears all over the palace and all over the city, and any one of them could be behind this."

Ryaela nodded. That made sense. It hadn't occurred to her just how many suspects there could be. Any one of them could be in the pay of someone who wanted her dead. And that gave her an idea.

"Then we keep the number involved in the plan to a minimum," Ryaela said. "I know you have a thousand plans to deal with this, but hear mine first."

"I'm all ears, my lady," Galeran smiled at her.

"You know as well as I do that the best way to lure someone out of hiding is to offer them what they want," Ryaela said. "So I intend to do just that."

"Ryaela, they almost killed you," Galeran gripped her hand tightly. "If you try to offer yourself up as bait, they might succeed."

"They would kill you in a second," Ryaela shot back. "I can't let you get hurt when their vendetta is against me alone. Please, Galeran, I can't let you get involved. If this assassin finds out you're going in with me, they might strike you first."

She covered his hand with her free one and silently begged him not to let his stubbornness cloud his judgment. He was the Crown Prince and she would not let him throw his life away for hers. She cared about him too damn much.

"My lady," Galeran said softly. "I know this might be a liability, but the thought of you facing them alone again worries me. They stuck two ghost daggers in you. You nearly bled out right in front of me. At least keep someone on standby if something goes wrong. Maybe you should have a bodyguard."

"Gods no! Giving me a bodyguard might scare them off. You saw how they reacted when you and Nila came to my rescue," Ryaela said. "I need be alone for this. That's what draws them out."

"You're a stubborn fool," Galeran said. "At least keep Nila and me on standby if you won't trust anyone else. I'm useless enough that they'll probably strike anyway."

"Who's the stubborn fool now?" Ryaela asked with a smirk. "I doubt I'll need you and Nila on standby, but if it makes you feel better, I'll accept. The Bastard got two strikes on me, I need some payback. Besides, after nearly killing me, they're probably going to get cocky."

"I hope you're right," Galeran said.

"Shut up, Galeran, I'm always right," Ryaela snorted.

Galeran laughed before flashing that crooked grin she liked so much. "Forgive me, my lady, how could I be so forgetful. I think the anxiety of being without you is getting to me."

Ryaela laughed along with him for a few moments before they both went quiet. She looked down at their hands again before looking up at Galeran's face. He looked unsure of what he was supposed to do next.

"I...I should probably send for Nila," Galeran said. His voice was halting, like there was something else he would rather be telling her. "She needs to be informed of this plan."

"Oh, of course," Ryaela answered. Disappointment pricked at her chest even though she wasn't sure what she was disappointed about.

Galeran rose but didn't let go of her hand. He stood there for a few moments and right when Ryaela was about to ask if something was wrong, he leaned down and kissed her cheek. Ryaela's eyes went wide as Galeran let go of her hand and gave her a shy smile. Her heart thumped against her ribs as Galeran left the room.

"Do you think The Bastard is going to show?" Nila asked Ryaela as they put on their armor.

"If I'm truly the target, they will," Ryaela replied. "Every other arrogant bastard we've faced has tried to take what they want as soon they think it's being offered."

"I'm worried about this one, Ryaela," Nila said. "This assassin is worse than any of our past adversaries ever were. They can look like anyone for heaven's sake!"

"I'm aware," Ryaela replied. "I can't believe how close they were to having us. We almost convicted Prince Dalziel of high treason."

"I'm glad Prince Galeran was able to drop his bias and look at facts," Nila said. "I would not have wanted to be the one to break the news to Serae that her charge is getting executed."

"I know," Ryaela chuckled. "Speaking of, I take it that His Majesty hasn't been too much trouble?"

"Drop the act, Ryaela, I know you call him by his first name," Nila snorted. "And he's fine. Broody, but fine. Kind of like you for the last two days."

"I have not been broody!" Ryaela shot back.

"You have, and don't pretend I don't know why," Nila gave her a long-suffering look. "I really hope this blasted assassin comes out of their hole because you and Galeran need to have a talk."

Ryaela felt a blush as she thought about Galeran's lips against her cheek. She'd been too busy to speak with him much since that night. She transferred her guard duties to Nila and taken her palace patrol to hunt for the assassin. Ryaela always managed to catch his eye whenever she passed him. He always smiled and begged her to be careful with those dark eyes of his. Ryaela hoped she'd managed to let him know that she would.

"Yes, yes, I know," Ryaela said with a wave of her hand. "And we will. As soon as this assassin business is finished."

"You'd better, otherwise you're both going to be nightmares," Nila replied, finishing the last buckle on her breastplate. "Anyway, I'm off to see to His Majesty. We'll be waiting for your call."

"Thanks, Nila," Ryaela smiled at her. "Good luck."

"Thanks, Ryaela, you too," Nila saluted before leaving the room.

Ryaela took a deep breath and finished with her armor. It was time to hunt. The assassin had been quiet for the last few days. She thought for certain they would try to finish her off in her sleep, while she was laid up with her wounds, but they hadn't. That was when Ryaela realized there was more to this vendetta than simple vengeance. This assassin had something to prove. They didn't just want to take her out, they wanted to win. Ryaela couldn't help but feel a twinge of respect for them.

The first few hours of patrolling the palace halls showed nothing out of the ordinary, and nothing out of place. The breeze sighed through the trees outside, and brought a chill through a nearby open window. Ryaela couldn't tell if it was because Oranteon was displeased or simply because fall was coming. She shivered regardless, and gripped her axe tightly.

She almost didn't see the shadow. Ryaela whipped around at the last second to parry the assassin's double knife strike with the handle of her axe.

"You're out early today, aren't you?" Ryaela said.

The assassin snorted before spinning out of the way and whipping one of their ghost daggers at her. Ryaela side-stepped and the blade clattered across the floor.

"I must admit, I'm surprised you're still here," she went on. "I thought for sure you'd just murder me in my sleep and be done with it. It's actually kind of refreshing to meet an assassin willing to look into their adversary's face."

The assassin stalked around her, the ghost dagger they'd thrown reappearing in their hand. They moved on the balls of their feet and their eyes never left Ryaela's face. For the first time, they weren't mocking.

Ryaela lunged first, trying to drive them towards one of the open windows. When The Bastard leapt back, Ryaela adjusted her swing, nearly clipping their shoulder. The assassin's eyes went wide as they braced themselves against a pillar between two of the windows. They pushed off the pillar and launched themselves into the air, both daggers aimed at Ryaela's shoulders. She ducked low and rammed the top of her axe upwards, slamming it into the assassin's stomach and forcing them up and over her head. Ryaela heard the air leave The Bastard's lungs in a gasp as they hit the ground in a haphazard roll. Ryaela smirked as she spun and rushed them down. The Bastard looked up at her from their crouch, the cloth covering the bottom half of their face slipped down. Ryaela stopped dead in her tracks.

"E-Elsharra?" Ryaela almost couldn't make her voice work. "Elsharra, what the hell are you doing?"

Elsharra stared back at her with hate as cold as winter in her dark eyes. "Taking what's mine."

She lunged at Ryaela, daggers nearly a blur. Ryaela only just managed to parry the blows with the handle of her axe.

"What?" Ryaela asked. "Why?"

She blocked another of Elsharra's swings and kicked her backwards. "Why are you doing this? What will killing me give you?"

Elsharra glared at her before rising to the balls of her feet and creeping around her. "They listen to you, the entire royal family. You've got them in your pocket! The Crown Prince defers to you like a dog! What do you think he'll do when he becomes king? A high council seat? High general? He'll be falling over himself to give you whatever you want!"

Ryaela felt a surge of anger and she rushed Elsharra again. Galeran was not a dog! He would give her a seat because she godsdamned earned it!

Elsharra ducked under the swinging axe blade and danced out of the way. "I outrank you, Vaeliadatyr!" she spat. "And what do they give me? Nothing! A pat on the head, a few more gold pieces. Do they ever consider me for the open council seats? No! Not when they have Ryaela the Almighty!" She lunged at Ryaela's side, blades flashing like lightning.

Ryaela barely managed to back out of the way. She felt the blades scrape against her armor. "That's what this is about?" Ryaela snarled. "You betrayed your home and your people because you didn't get what you think you deserve?"

"I don't think it, Vaeliadatyr," Elsharra bared her teeth. "I know it."

"You forfeited everything when you took up a blade against me!" Ryaela shot back. "Who are you working for?"

"What does it matter?" Elsharra snapped. "You'll be dead."

Ryaela swiped at her with her axe, driving her back across the hallway. She smirked as she felt her axe catch on Elsharra's arm.

"Who are you working for?" Ryaela demanded.

"You needn't worry," Elsharra replied as she backed away. "Oranteon will be in capable hands. Your beloved prince might even get to live."

A roar tore from Ryaela's throat and she hurled herself at Elsharra. Fear flashed in Elsharra's eyes. She dodged Ryaela's first strike but the second cut deep into her shoulder. Elsharra let out a pained grunt as she staggered backwards. Blood oozed from her shoulder and dripped on the floor. Ryaela bared her teeth and slashed at her again, rage giving her wings. She buried her axe deep into Elsharra's side and used the swing to hurl her to the ground. Elsharra let out a strangled gasp and coughed up blood. Ryaela felt a vicious satisfaction as she pulled her axe from Elsharra's flesh. She crouched beside the gasping spymaster and rested her axe against her chest.

"Not so smug now, are you?" Ryaela asked. "Who are you working for? Tell me and I can guarantee you your life."

Elsharra let out a wet cough and spat blood on the floor next to Ryaela's foot. She looked back up at Ryaela and smirked. "It doesn't matter. You're surrounded and so is your pet prince. Oranteon will soon choose more worthy occupants. I hope you live to see it turn its back on you."

The wind blew a frigid hiss from outside and Elsharra shuddered like she'd been slapped. Ryaela snarled and punched Elsharra in the face. Her eyes rolled back into her skull and she went limp. She was worth more to them alive than dead. Ryaela wished she could just kill her and be done with it.

The trees rustled and whispered beside the windows. Ryaela took a deep breath and let it out slowly. Oranteon was in her blood, in every fiber of her. As long as she drew breath, she would fight for it.

"Surrounded, am I?" Ryaela muttered as she tore a sleeve from Elsharra's mottled assassin's clothing and used it to staunch the blood from her side. "Let them come. I hope you live to see me rise."

Glamor and Thread

Stephanie Smith

Five minutes before the first meeting of the day, Irene sat in a corner of the convention hall, facing the battery. She had supervised when the workmen had rolled it in that morning. When Irene hosted these assemblies, she liked to be thorough. The battery was impressive in its own right. The geode was four feet tall, full of spiky orange crystals. Irene had seen it for the first time when she was fourteen, and even back then it had astounded her. She had been impressed that the earth could spit out something so jaggedly beautiful.

After over a decade of assemblies, Irene could just make out the thin lines of magic spiraling and stretching out of the battery, thinner than silk thread, so white it seemed to glow. The effect was dazzling and strangely nostalgic.

The battery in Florence had been nice too. Its crystals were afternoon-horizon blue, and it was about two feet taller. Still, when Irene saw that battery she felt nothing but awe. This battery made Irene feel like she was home. Right now, Irene needed that more than anything.

Slowly, Irene took a sip of her coffee and forced her mind to go blank. Between the assembly and her show and Regina not coming and Kallie coming and the whole scandal that had happened a few months back, there was a lot to deal with.

Still, there was a window not too far away. Irene got to watch a post-daybreak Midwestern sky in one of her best suits, which she'd enchanted to feel cozier than a fleece blanket. The lines of magic glinted on her suit, as intricate and delicate as a spiderweb.

Irene took another sip. It was plain coffee, nonmagic. The food vendors didn't usually set up until about 8 AM. This coffee was still good, just not as good as the coffee she would get later in the day.

Her phone buzzed, and she checked it immediately. Thankfully, it wasn't an emergency. Kallie was just responding to Irene's text from last night. She had the makeup kit together. All clear.

Then, before Irene could get back into a calm empty space again, Alice rounded the corner, holding her own stainless steel thermos. Her black hair was back in a ponytail, and she was wearing the platform boots that made her about as tall as Irene. Alice wasn't in her full makeup, not yet. Even with magic, costume makeup was costume makeup, and it was a little too early in the morning to apply it.

Irene understood. She planned on changing out of the suit once the assembly really started. This was a time for setting up, not showing off.

Alice stopped in her tracks, but Irene waved her over. Her five minutes were over anyway. Alice still looked guilty when she sat down next to Irene.

"Morning," Alice said.

"Morning."

For a few seconds they sipped coffee in sleepy silence.

"Know I said this last night, but I'm glad you're back," said Alice casually.

Irene nodded. "I'm glad to be back. Italy was nice, but it's not home, you know?"

Alice shook her head once and sighed. "Maybe the timing was for the best. The Terry James thing was a nightmare."

"I know." Irene had watched the whole thing blow up online while she was overseas.

Silence crept over them again. This time it was graver, sadder.

Most people came into the magic community when they were teenagers. Older people, like Irene's mentor Regina, were in charge of guiding newcomers through the community and teaching them how to use their gifts. Irene, who was trans, homeless, and desperate to be magic, couldn't have asked for a better mentor.

The mentor system was older than the assemblies. It was a tradition as sacred as magic itself. So when a pupil sued a mentor for statutory rape, it was bound to be messy.

While Irene was studying abroad, a group of twelve women levied charges against Terry James. Three of the lawsuits were from his former pupils. The youngest woman was barely eighteen.

Terry James was in his late forties now, a handful of years younger than Regina. He had done important things in the community, and he had some high-profile friends. The backlash against those women had been viscerally ugly.

It had been an awful handful of months. Irene was simultaneously glad and regretful that she'd been in out of the country for most of it.

Irene shifted in her seat and said, quietly, "Regina's not going to be here for most of the day."

Alice blinked. "But she flew in last night, right? I remember seeing her at the hotel bar."

Irene wondered whether Alice had noticed the nail polish. Last night when Regina had flown in she hadn't been wearing any. In the last few months Regina's nails had been a solid pale pink; Irene saw them during their video calls. Out of everything, the nail polish was Irene's biggest hint that Regina was not doing well.

"Regina's coming to my show. It's my study abroad exhibition, she wouldn't miss it for the world," Irene explained. "But that's the only thing she wants to see *here*, you know? She says the assemblies have gotten nastier."

Alice looked like she understood. Irene could have stopped there, but she'd wanted to confide in somebody about this.

"I get it. You spend like forty years with these people, working and trying to make things better. You start thinking it's safe. Then something happens, and it turns out the bad stuff wasn't ever gone, it was just *hiding*.

"Regina's been really passionate about defending those women, but lately some of the people she's argued with have been getting—" Irene searched for a word "—personal."

Alice's sadness and indignation and fury passed across her face in quick succession. She pinched the bridge of her nose and muttered, "Jesus *Christ.*"

"So she's not coming," Irene finished lamely.

"No wonder," Alice said, leaning back so forcefully she hit the back of the chair with a thud. "I mean, sure, people have been assholes about it but not that bad." A thought occurred to Alice and she looked sharply at Irene. "Are you worried?"

Irene shrugged. "Should I be?"

To her credit, Alice thought about it before she said, "I don't think so. Don't get me wrong, people have said some disgusting things, but the assemblies themselves have been peaceful so far. And since this is your assembly, I think it'll be okay."

Hearing that made Irene feel a little better. "Thanks."

She checked her phone, stood up, and said, "We better get to that meeting."

Alice stood up followed her to one of the center's many conference rooms. The head volunteer, Jack, was waiting at the door. He was talking with another volunteer with blonde hair and a t-shirt. When the volunteer saw Irene she handed her a croissant.

Irene could taste the magic in it, the vibrant richness that made everything else melt away when she took the first bite. Irene made a note to ask Jack that girl's name, because she was going places.

Two hours passed in a blur of changing into new clothes, greeting people, checking rooms, setting up podiums and courses, settling small disputes, ordering around interns, checking up on panelists and sending a mass email with directions and parking rules (even though all of that information was already on the website), and then answering the texts of the people who didn't check their email.

Irene didn't find herself alone again until 9 AM, sitting on a freezing bench in an empty train station. She was nursing another cup of coffee, this one with a pretty heavy enchantment. It tasted only slightly flatter now that she was away from the convention and the battery, but she could still feel it. Even though she'd been drinking coffee since this morning, every sip felt as bold and new as her first drink of the day.

An unfathomably cold breeze cut through Irene's duffle coat, and her phone buzzed in her pocket. She let herself wait a full minute before she checked it. Irene expected the text to be from Jack or Alice, but it was Kallie, saying that she had boarded the train and she would be there in about twenty minutes.

Irene replied immediately, said she was already on the platform and she couldn't wait. Kallie said that she was excited, and Irene said that she was excited too.

That wasn't a lie, but the conversation had left Irene feeling apprehensive, guilty. She felt like she'd made some subtle mistake and the horrible unforeseen consequence was already on its way.

Irene knew the feeling was baseless. Kallie loved the idea of working on a fashion show with Irene; she wouldn't have agreed to it if she didn't. Kallie was also flattered that Irene wanted her to be one of the models. If Kallie was okay with that, then there was no reason to be upset.

As for the assembly, Kallie was about as accepting as anybody could be about the existence of magic. It wasn't like she'd have a problem believing in it when she got there.

Irene still stewed in this feeling for several minutes before Alice walked up to the bench.

Alice seemed oddly lazy and feline thanks to her makeup. Her face was covered in tiger stripes, nose flattened and widened into a snout. Irene noticed that Alice's teeth were sharp, but that was hardly surprising; there was a special place in Alice's heart for prosthetic fangs.

"Hey," Alice said, settling down next to Irene on the bench. She gestured at the coffee. "How much have you had?"

"This is my fifth cup, I think."

"Your ability to run on nothing but sugar and caffeine is enviable."

"Thank you. It's a talent."

"Seriously, though, are you all right? Have you had anything substantial to eat this morning?"

"I had a muffin. And a ham and cheese croissant."

Alice looked surprised. "Thank goodness. You usually forget to eat anything."

Honestly, Irene had forgotten. Right after someone yelled at her over charging thirty dollars for admission to certain events, and right before Jack let her know that the vendors in the food sector needed help setting up, Irene had started feeling weak and unsteady. The only thing that kept her from swooning was the blonde volunteer, who swept by with the croissant just in time.

The girl's pastries were enchanted, no doubt about that, but her sense of timing was uncanny enough that it couldn't be anything but magic. She was probably like Jack, who could feel out awkward moments from several feet away.

"I had help," she admitted. "That blonde volunteer with the pastries, she's a godsend. I'm definitely asking her to my next event. Do you know her?"

"Yeah. Well, not personally, but a lot of people know about her now. That's Liza Schafield." When Irene still looked confused Alice clarified, "One of Terry's pupils."

Irene sat in silence, partially shocked, partially lost in thought. Finally she asked, "Has she been doing all right?"

Alice shrugged. "A lot of assembly hosts have blacklisted her, which you know, sucks, but she's been getting by. Some bakers still like her, since she uses and promotes their stuff. And Jack's been nice to her at least."

Irene made a decision. "I'm asking her to all of my assemblies then. Maybe she can be my head volunteer if she's comfortable with it. We could also start doing some panels on sexual harassment in the community?"

Alice shifted again. "The panels, definitely. We need more discussions about this. I'm not sure how Liza feels about being in the spotlight these days, though."

"Yeah," Irene said glumly. She pinched the bridge of her nose. "God, inviting Kallie into all of this feels especially messed up."

"It is what it is." When Alice saw Irene's face she added, "I actually think it's a good thing you're working with her on the show. I mean, the whole scandal started because of mentor-pupil relationships and how we treat them. I think that bringing in an outsider as a partner is a good precedent. Show the community that there are other ways to bring people in."

"Yeah," Irene sighed.

"And Kallie's excited about this, right?"

"We've been planning this since I finished the first dress. She's really interested in working at a fashion show. I think this is good exposure for her."

"Definitely. Good for you too, considering how talented Kallie is with makeup."

"Right? It's mutually beneficial. I'm really excited about it."

They talked until the train pulled up to the station and Kallie stepped off, wearing a belted tan skater dress under an olive bolero.

Seeing Kallie in person was surreal. Irene had online friends, but she got to see most of them at assemblies two or three times a year. The last time she'd seen Kallie had been over a year ago, at a fashion blogging conference. Now Kallie was hugging her, smelling faintly of peppermint and foundation, and Irene so happy she couldn't process it.

Then Irene stepped back and noticed Kallie's makeup. Irene had expected that Kallie would do something jaw-dropping and colorful, especially considering that she was the last model in the show. Instead her makeup was sensible, her eyeshadow was a sedated sort of brown, and her eyeliner and blush were subtle as a murmur. Irene didn't work with makeup, but she could tell that whatever Kallie's makeup did near the battery, it wouldn't turn heads in the traditional sense.

In Kallie's online tutorials, Irene had seen Kallie pull off bright blue eyeshadow and purple lip stain, weaving intricate nets of magic across her face. At first, Irene couldn't believe that Kallie didn't know about magic. It wasn't shyness, couldn't be.

Two things calmed Irene down. First, she could still see the lines of magic on her face, so there was an enchantment there. Second, this was Kallie. She probably had a plan.

"Glad you're here," Kallie said, once she was done hugging Alice. She looked at the two of them, eyes wide. "Alice, you look fantastic! And God, Irene, your dress!"

"Thank you," Irene said. Alice was beaming. She should have looked carnivorous, what with the makeup, but instead she just seemed really happy.

"Seriously though. How did you manage those stripes? And Irene," she gestured at the whole dress, "you look like a mermaid. The ruffles are perfect, I don't know what you were talking about!"

Irene preened. The dress was part of the project that had eaten every spare hour she spent in Italy, the project that inspired the fashion show. Irene had worked with her fellow designer and host Vanessa for months. The two of them were compatibly crazy, and their work had been a zealous, all-nighter kind of fun. When she'd got back to the states, Irene had slept for about a week straight.

While she was working, Irene had sent Kallie updates, pictures of dresses in progress, midnight rants about hems and colors and how none of the ruffles ever looked like waves. However, Irene had kept this particular project a surprise. Once she realized that this was going to be her best dress, Irene wanted Kallie to see it in person.

"Let's get going," Irene said, beaming. As they started walking off the platform she explained, "I know we have an hour before show setup even starts, but if you'd like we can take a walk around the convention center. It shouldn't be all business, you know?"

"That sounds good," said Kallie. "From what you guys told me, the assembly sounds really fun."

It seemed like Kallie was diplomatically avoiding the subject of the magic itself. That was all right. She'd see it when they got there.

"First things first though," Alice said seriously, "Kallie, have you eaten?"

Kallie shrugged guiltily and confessed, "I, um, I was running late and didn't have time to grab my granola bar."

Alice groaned. "You two are killing me."

* * *

Kallie took her first experience near the battery well, all things considered. It helped that the changes were relatively slow from an outsider's perspective. From Kallie's point of view, Alice's makeup slowly turned real, becoming more textured than it had before. Irene's dress rippled and flowed like the entire sea was draped across her body.

Unfortunately, when Irene looked at Kallie, her worst suspicions were confirmed. Between the neutral colors and the bright light of her magic, Kallie's face turned into a blur. It was like when Irene looked at Kallie, the part of Irene's brain that was supposed to register faces completely blanked. In fact, if she looked away too long, she tended to forgot that Kallie was there.

Alice gave her a mirror to check it out. At first Kallie was amazed, and then she was positively elated.

"It's real! It's real!" She grinned, or Irene thought she grinned. "My God, I thought you guys were kidding but it's real! This is so cool! Ugh, and it's going to look so good in the show too!" When she saw Irene's expression, she said, "I'm serious. This will look great with the dress you picked out, trust me."

Irene smiled. Seeing her this happy was agonizingly pleasant.

Alice led them to the food stands. Irene was more interested in the bakery than anything else, but she bought some sushi so Alice wouldn't shake her head and lecture about protein. Kallie bought a breakfast sandwich and salad. Alice had already eaten, but she got a smoothie just to have something to drink.

Kallie groaned as she bit into the sandwich. "This is so good. How is this so good?"

"Magic," Irene said. She wanted to sound totally serious, but it came out just wry enough for Kallie to chuckle.

"Really though," Kallie said. "It's a little hard to believe that a rock can make all this happen."

Irene shrugged. "Believe me, we know. If you'd like, we could hit one of the seminars tonight. Someone's presenting a research paper on the chemical analysis of the battery."

"There are articles online too," Alice added. "What's the theory these days? Is radiation still in vogue or have we jumped back to molecular nonsense?"

"I'll take molecules over radiation any day." Irene said, grappling with her chopsticks. "Radiation theories feel like a rehash of the cosmic ray theories from the sixties."

"Aw, come on. If magic is real, comic book physics can be real too," Kallie teased.

"But that's the thing." Irene knew she was taking the question way too seriously, but she wanted to make a point. "Superhero stories with those physics are about one person, or one group of people, becoming better than everyone else. But that's not how the battery works, it's not how magic works. We're all special, but only *slightly* special, no matter how close we stand to the battery. So applying the superhero mindset is kind of harmful, considering that magic is egalitarian."

Alice had been nodding along to the speech—she'd heard it often enough. "You're not wrong about that. Still, radiation might be the answer."

"Then I will be fundamentally disappointed in the battery and magic itself forever."

Irene popped some ginger in her mouth, checked the clock, and sighed. "Kallie, I was going to show you all the different sections of the convention, but I don't think we'll have time."

"Sections?" Kallie asked.

"Yeah," Irene explained. "Everyone has different gifts, so there are different sections. Like Jack—I'll have to introduce you to Jack soon, he's nice—Jack's magic is more social. Like he can tell when people are having a private moment and he shouldn't butt in.

So the social section is made up of people like Jack, and they give you advice and play games and things.

"Then there's the clairvoyant section, where people who are really good at guessing the weather can give you forecasts and people can tell you where to look for missing stuff, things like that, and then there's the athletic section—"

Irene kept explaining. Thankfully, Kallie looked more or less entertained, and Alice added bits of information when necessary.

By the time they were done eating, they definitely didn't have enough time to walk around the whole center. Instead, Kallie and Irene decided to get a head start on preparing for the show, but they would make a quick stop at the battery first.

The first time Irene saw the t-shirt, she thought it was an accident. She thought she had read it wrong.

Then she noticed someone else wearing the same shirt, down to the color, sleeve length and font. This time she read the full thing, and it said, "Terry James Legal Defense Squad."

With rising dread, Irene noticed more and more people wearing those shirts. She sent a text out to the volunteer group when she thought Alice and Kallie were occupied.

To be honest, she wasn't sure how to handle it yet. There weren't any rules against wearing shirts with divisive slogans, but there hadn't been any reason for those kinds of rules before. If the t-shirts included an open threat, that would be another situation, but potential implications weren't enough to get them thrown out.

The volunteers checked in. Liza, though, didn't say anything. It wasn't unusual: no one had to respond to every text. Still, Irene wondered in retrospect if she should have included her in the group message at all.

Irene worried about it right up until they were in front of the battery. Kallie let out a little dazzled breath. Irene looked at Kallie, then, trying to see past the makeup. She wished she could see Kallie's smile.

Irene held her breath and tried not to fidget as Kallie walked forward. They'd staged the fashion show in one of the ballrooms, so Kallie didn't have a catwalk or a proper platform to work with. Hopefully the intimate setting would work in Kallie's favor.

The audience had been demure to fawning so far. No one would come to a host's event and then openly mock their work. Still, Kallie was a literal unknown, so there was no telling how the crowd would react to her.

Kallie nailed it. As soon as the crowd saw Kallie there were gasps and murmurs almost as loud as the background music. It was impossible to tell whether that made Kallie smile or not, because from the front row her face was as blurry and subtle as the blend of grays and greens and blues on the dress. She was right, that makeup was perfect for this outfit.

Irene should have been basking in the triumph. Instead she was grappling with herself. There was something underneath her happiness, too strong to be trusted. She'd pushed down that feeling when it came up before. This time it stayed.

After the show, Irene mingled, and thankfully didn't cross paths with Kallie. She did, however, nearly walk into beaming Regina.

Regina stood in heels that made her tower over everyone else in the crowd. It wasn't so much that she was wearing a royal blue sheath dress and gold bangles; Regina dressed aggressively well whether she felt like it or not. It was the fact that her nails were indigo, with a little silver rocket on one pinkie and Saturn on the other. Irene grinned and hugged her.

Regina told her how fantastic the show was, and then asked, "So who was that seventh model? Was she your new pupil?"

"What?" The question was so direct it felt like it had stopped Irene's heart for a second.

"Your new pupil. You couldn't have staged a better debut. She was in the best dress, she had the best makeup, she was the last one onstage."

"She's not my pupil," Irene explained. "We worked together on this project, that's all," Irene said, trying to keep her voice steady. "Kallie is really talented, she did her own makeup."

"Really? That's fantastic! I have to meet her then."

"You definitely do," Irene said, trying not to sound too relieved. "She's amazing."

"If you don't mind my asking, though," Regina said quietly, "If she's not your pupil, are you two, um, together?"

Irene froze.

"I'm sorry," Regina said hastily, looking at Irene's face. "Look, don't listen to me. Forget I said anything."

When that didn't help, Regina leaned in and said, "I'm so sorry, Irene. I didn't mean to hit a nerve."

"No, no, it's fine," Irene said, as if she still didn't look absolutely stunned. "I just, ah—"

"—Need to go," Regina finished. She patted Irene's shoulder guiltily and said, "I'll make your excuses. I really am sorry, Irene. If you want to talk about it later, I'll be here for you."

Irene nodded numbly, then walked away, out of the ballroom. She tried to go slow but by the time she reached the door she was at a run.

Once she got out of the room she just stood by the door and tried to calm down. People were milling around in the hall around her, and the door swung open and closed almost constantly. For a few minutes she just stood outside and breathed, hiding in the stream of people.

It was stupid to run out like that. If she could make it back before too much time had passed, it would be fine. It was possible no one would even notice.

Then Alice walked through the door, and things were no longer fine.

"Are you okay?" Alice looked legitimately worried.

Irene tried to look nonchalant, like she was just leaning on the wall and watching the people walking by. "What? No."

"Irene, Regina told me to go talk to you. Something happened."

Irene sighed. "It was nothing, I just overreacted."

"To what?"

If only she didn't have to say it. Irene wished she didn't have to say it, but Alice wouldn't stop looking at her. "Regina thought," Irene began slowly, "that Kallie was, um, my pupil."

A small, relieved laugh escaped Alice. "Yeah, well, people would think that. It's all right, though, Regina would understand. Was that all?"

"Um," Irene said. She paused, then squirmed under Alice's eyes. "When Regina thought that Alice wasn't my pupil, she, um, she asked if we were together."

"Oh," said Alice. She didn't get it at first. "Well, that's like the mentor thing, all we have to do is set people straight."

Irene didn't have anything to say to that. In a few seconds, Alice got it.

"Irene," Alice said, entirely too gingerly, entirely too gently.

"Kallie's straight," Irene said, and it sounded too much like a death sentence. She tried to sound more energetic when she said, "Kallie's straight."

"Oh, buddy," Alice said, which was not making things any better.

69

"No, it's okay. We're two professionals who work together," Irene insisted. "She's straight, I'm not, I know that. I can get over myself."

"Irene," Alice had her hand on her forehead. "Irene, this is *not* okay. You've got a crush on Kallie."

"It's fine. So long as I don't make Kallie uncomfortable—"

"Then you'll feel like shit but everything will still be *fine*," Alice snapped. "Irene, this is *monumentally* bad. You're setting yourself up to get hurt, and like it or not you're going to end up hurting Kallie too. What are you going to do if she finds out? Or will she just 'never find out' and you'll be stuck pining until you can't take it anymore? Jesus, Irene, you're *smart*, how did you even get into this?"

"I thought I could handle it," Irene snapped back. "I thought that fine, maybe I can ignore this stupid halfhearted romance thing to work with someone who's really talented and also an awesome friend. But sure, fine, you're right and I'm wrong, I'm an idiot—"

"You're not an idiot," Alice said sharply. Then softer, she said, "Weren't you listening? You're smart, you're one of the smartest people I know. It's just that sometimes you pretend that the way you feel doesn't matter. I like you, and I like Kallie. I don't want to see either of you hurt."

When Irene didn't answer, Alice said, "I am sorry. Feelings are terrible."

Then Alice was hugging her, and Irene needed it so she hugged back. Then Alice tensed and Irene pulled back, saw that Alice was watching something in the middle distance.

"What?"

"Nothing," Alice said, too quickly. But Irene followed her eyes and saw someone moving away, someone with a green bolero and a tan dress.

"God damn it."

Irene did not ask how it could get any worse. She pointedly didn't. It was tempting fate.

Regardless, at that moment Jack texted to ask whether anyone had seen Liza in the past thirty minutes. And one by one, people texted back to say that no, no they hadn't.

They looked for Liza. Judging by t-shirts alone Liza had about twenty people at the assembly who were, at the very least, not going to be friendly towards her. Kallie was alone, and that sucked, but odds were people wouldn't actively target her. For all Irene knew, Liza had been in danger from the beginning.

Irene found time, between talking to volunteers and organizing search parties, to hate herself. She should have called a meeting the minute she saw the t-shirts, Kallie or no. And God, the whole Kallie business. That stung too much to think about.

So Irene didn't think about it. She organized the volunteers into teams to comb the convention center. It was possible that Liza was just not answering her phone, she said, and somewhere in the convention. Or she could have been in a bathroom, or a conference room if she didn't feel safe in the open.

(And in the meantime, if Alice happened to be the one to text Kallie, then that would be best. Irene wouldn't know what to say.)

Irene debated whether the whole convention should know that Liza was missing. It would help, in theory, but it could also backfire spectacularly, especially if Liza was just having phone problems.

There wouldn't be any announcements yet. However, there was an entire section of clairvoyants who Irene could ask, quietly, about where she might find a person she was looking for.

One clairvoyant told her to look in her purse, which was unlikely (though she did find a crumpled-up twenty dollar bill). Another one told Irene to look in the bathroom she had visited in the morning, and all Irene found was her spare hotel key.

Then, twenty minutes later, someone found Liza in a conference room. She wasn't alone.

Irene stood in the doorway, looking in on a wide oval table, a whiteboard, and two women in swivel chairs who had faces that she couldn't quite focus on. One of the women was wearing an olive bolero and a tan dress. The other one was holding an empty pastry basket. There was an open makeup palette on the table, and a brush in Kallie's hand. Irene's heart skipped.

"I'm sorry," Liza said immediately, standing up as more people funneled into the room. "My phone died, and I was just—I'm sorry."

"No, no, you're fine," Irene said breathlessly. "We were just worried. It's okay now."

She assured Liza several more times that everything was fine, she didn't have to worry, it was okay. The other volunteers left the room, seeing that there was nothing left to do. Jack hugged Liza and they walked out together, talking quietly. At some point it was just the three of them left: Alice, Irene, and Kallie.

Irene cleared her throat and stepped towards the door, but Kallie said her name. When she turned back to look at Kallie Alice slipped out the door. Irene got a text that said: *Waiting outside. Talk to her.*

For a few seconds, Irene stood at one end of the room and Kallie stood at the other. Apparently neither of them knew what to say.

Irene sat down next to Kallie, because it was something to do. She said, "It was good of you, hanging out with Liza like that."

Kallie shrugged. "It was the least I could do."

Irene shifted. "Did someone—?"

"I don't think so. I think people were just giving her dirty looks and she felt really upset. I didn't get the whole story, but we talked a little. She said she wanted people to stop looking at her. Like I said, it was the least I could do."

Irene sighed and pinched the bridge of her nose. "God. She shouldn't have to *hide*. We need to fix this."

"What is going on?"

When Irene finished her summary, Kallie was quiet for a minute. "Well, I shouldn't be too surprised. That kind of stuff is everywhere," she said in a small voice.

"Yeah," Irene sighed. Her heart broke when she heard the way Kallie said it. "Just because we're magic doesn't mean we're not really, really messed up."

"If you want to go home, I'd understand," Irene added. "Between this and...the other thing."

"Do you want me to leave?"

Irene blinked, swallowed the "no" that immediately came to mind. Instead she said, "This isn't about what I want."

"Yes, it is," Kallie said simply, still quiet but looking Irene straight in the eye. For a minute Irene could see her full face.

"I'm sorry," Irene said.

"That's not what I meant," Kallie said quickly. "I mean, I heard what you said and it sounds...bad. I mean, that sort of thing hurts, and I don't want to hurt you."

"Hurt me?" For some reason that was the thing that finally made Irene blush. "God, I have a weird crush on you, invite you to an assembly that I'm hosting, ask you to my show, and you're worried about hurting *me*?"

"It's not weird," Kallie said. "And you didn't drag me here, I wanted to come! I like hanging out with you."

"What about now?" Irene asked glumly.

"Now," Kallie answered, looking at some spot on the floor. "Now I still want to hang out, but it'll be hard for you. I spent time pining over people, and it sucks. I like you, even if it's not like that. I don't want to make you feel bad just because of me."

Irene only halfway knew what to think. It was like slowly untangling a knot in a necklace chain, so small and dense she couldn't tell where to pull or what to loosen.

"I like this," Kallie said. "This assembly thing is amazing. I really want to see the rest of it. I also like working with you.

"But if that hurts you, then I can go home. I like you as a friend, but I really wouldn't be comfortable with anything else. So I would understand if you don't want to see me for a while."

Kallie looked at her. And Irene wasn't any closer to untying the knot, but it was time to pick an end of the chain and go with it, so she opened her mouth.

"I like you," she said simply. "A lot. And I don't want to get rid of a friendship that's important to me just because I like you too much. I also don't want to make you uncomfortable or put you in a bad place."

Kallie made a face. "You haven't."

"I know, and I won't. But I still have these feelings, and they aren't going to go away just because I want them to. And I know that. I also know that being in denial about that can get really unhealthy."

Kallie nodded. Encouraged, Irene went on.

75

"But if this is about what I want, then if you're okay with it, I'd like to hang out with you and Alice for the rest of the day."

"I'm okay with that."

"Yeah. And we'll take it from there?"

"Sounds good to me."

Kallie offered her hand. Irene took it. They left the conference room together, and joined Alice outside.

Magnifikat

Emma Van Dyke

Mahter Magnifikat swept into the church (a crumbling old cube, standing lopsided as a gravestone in the salt marshes) just before dusk. Mahter's veil was her herald, billowing through the open door in the frigid wind. The veil was an alarming shade of red, covering her from headdress to train. It spiraled in the breeze like a bead of blood dropped into still water.

Mahter appeared in the doorway alone. She never required a retinue.

A Magnifikat of the Potentate could show her face, if she chose. Mahter did choose, though most people would rather she didn't. She had livid brown eyes, and cheekbones like a witch. The Magnifikat's slender eyebrows perpetually arched up, in disbelief or mockery, her thin dark lips twisting to emphasize her disappointment in the world at large.

The Pahters turned around in their seats when they heard her footsteps. Most of them blanched, and turned back around to face the sanctuary of the church, which doubled as an auction block when necessary. They lowered their bidding cards to their laps. Four of them got up and left. It was best to be gone from the places where Mahter Magnifikat bought her Mechaneet.

Everyone knew, of course, that the Magnifikat was part of the Church and the Potentate. She was well-praised and venerated by the Glorifikarum for her work.

They kept their eyes forward. They didn't move an inch.

The auctioneer, a half-blind runaway catcher with eight teeth to his name and a patch of greying rot on his scalp, didn't seem to notice the most notorious figure in the Potentate standing back in the shadows. He was occupied with the last sale of the day.

A Mechaneet with a magnificent collection of scars kicked and snarled as the auctioneer hauled her onto the platform with an arm around her waist. A standard Penitent model, with one missing arm. The auctioneer had already sold the arm separately: it was an ingenious and expensive contraption. At the swing and *click* of a hidden mechanism, the fingers spidered outward, and the glowing orb of a blaster started to crackle and hum.

Once the Mechaneet saw Mahter, who stood as still as a monolith carved from jet, her eyes widened with fear.

Mahter spared her a smile. Her eyes were old and cold. "First Mate Pecta," she said, her voice ringing off the moldering stone walls. "You've proven hard to find."

The Pahters craned their necks at the Mechaneet, suddenly interested. This common Penitent, an amber-eyed beauty with a silvered spine like any other—was Pecta herself. They exchanged silent glances, relief palpable between them. They had heard rumbles of something much, much more frightening.

Mahter stalked down the aisle, her veil whisking along the floor. She lifted it between finger and thumb to ascend the steps to the sanctuary. The auctioneer eyes widened once he realized who she was. He bowed deeply. Mahter raised a single finger in blessing, not looking at him. She reached out, and touched a scrape on Pecta's cheek. Though Pecta clamped her mouth shut and bore the Magnifikat's touch, her eyes blazed with anger.

The Magnifikat gestured, with a flick of her hand, to continue with the auction.

"Bidding—" the auctioneer's voice broke on the word, and he had to clear his throat and start again. "Bidding begins at sixty."

None of the Pahters even raised a card.

Mahter turned and surveyed all of the captured Mechaneet, nine of them in total, chained together on a bare bench. Nine pairs of amber, manufactured eyes, some downcast, some wide with fear or fury. The ones who dared to look up at her surveyed the red apparition before them.

When Mahter finally spoke, into the silence, her voice was quiet, and sharp. She made no effort to raise her voice. "All of them," she said, her finger still pressed against her lip in thought. "I'll take all of them."

A dripping silence filled the room. The auctioneer almost argued. Almost.

The Magnifikat descended the steps. Her red veil swept the stone, whispering over the floor. "I'll be waiting in my ship," she said. "Load them."

She turned back, halfway. The last of the evening light flared in the back window of the church, illuminating her. For a moment, it was as if the veil did not exist. Mahter was a woman

79

made of ink, obscured by the suggestion of red. "Pecta gets her own cell," she said.

In a swirl of skirts, she was gone.

The Pahters waited until they were sure she had left the church. Then, they erupted in a hail of complaints, standing up, raising their tickets high, and bombarding the auctioneer with demands for repayment, resale, remand.

Pecta stood above them all. She tipped her head up to the ceiling. Pecta knew runaways who, like her, had escaped from the worst places—from mines, from sludge pits, from the great and horrific Kathedral ships. Pecta had never met a single Mechaneet who had escaped from the Sisterhood of the Unseen Kompanion. She didn't even know what that strange, sinister name meant.

The ceiling had been painted in blue at one point—scraps of the color still clung to the rims of the arches. All else had been eaten by black rot.

The Abbey of the Order of the Unseen Kompanion was a lovely sight from space: a black ship, all planes and gleaming facets, petaled over with silver solar collectors on its dome. Everyone knew when the Sisterhood was in orbit around a planet: the ship was unmatched in the Potentate.

"It's a bit like having a Blast Boy as a manservant," commented one of the younger Pahters, standing at the viewport on the helm. Pahter Nuck had brought a full retinue, and even a

Magnapahter. Nuck thought it best to show the Mahter that she was being watched. Closely.

"Certainly, you want a Blast Boy when things go wrong," continued Pahter Pal. "But having one just looming, around you, all the time—" He gestured to the ship, currently in orbit around the moon of Kassus. "That gets unnerving."

Nuck narrowed his eyes at Pal.

Pal tucked his hands into his sleeves, bowed deeply, and left Nuck alone.

Nuck placed his hand back on the golden surface of the navigation screen. The ship itself was intelligent enough to negotiate a minor peace treaty, and certainly did not need Nuck's guidance. Still, Nuck liked to show the others that he had an eye on the proceedings.

That's what power was. Examining things in detail that others would prefer to believe simply worked well on their own. Nuck was not a young man, and he had been with the Aktuates a long time. He had learned that nothing worked well. Not if you looked hard enough.

The delegation of Pahters arrived precisely on time. Nuck and his retinue of twelve—a range of men, heads shaven, wearing identical sutayns—were directed by the ship's voice to the foyer of the Abbey. The receiving room featured a high, old-fashioned vaulted ceiling, painted a deep red, and a series of archways lining the courtyard. A canal of water shot through the center of the foyer, feeding several offshoots that trickled down to drains along the walkways. The garden was a dizzying knot of green, meant to be walked through while deep in prayer.

They waited from midmorning prayers past afternoon prayers. No one so much as stepped inside the room.

The Pahters of the retinue dissipated, some taking the opportunity to walk the maze and revel in the green—most of them had to spent their time on Kathedral ships, beautiful on the outside, but terribly cramped in living quarters. Magnapahter Lukis sat down on a bench and went to sleep.

Pahter Nuck stood, arms crossed, facing the red double doors that led into the inner sanctum. He didn't move.

When the double doors finally swung open, he straightened up. He clasped his hands behind his back, and gave a bow of the precise depth required for a Magnifikat.

The Sisters of the Unseen Kompanion were a fully Hidden Order: veiled from head to toe like red and faceless wraiths. They moved soundlessly through the door, arrayed themselves out, and bowed welcome.

Pahter Nuck rose. He realized that Mahter Magnifikat was not among them. He had wasted a bow on Sisters.

Nuck tipped his chin up. "You are incredibly late."

The Sisters were an imposing bunch: some tall, some short, all of them cloaked in red. Their veils were hearty and pleated. It was impossible to discern a single feature behind the cloth.

82

"Who are you, again?" he said to the Sister at the front of the pack.

The Sister reached inside a hidden fold in her robes, and then extended a gloved hand, card held between two gigantic fingers.

Pahter Nuck took it. He studied the neat print that covered the plain white side of the card.

> *Hello,*
>
> *My name is Sister Treesa. I am a member of the Sisterhood of the Unseen Kompanion. If you are reading this, you have tried to engage me in conversation. The Sisterhood of the Unseen Kompanion is a closed and silent order. Please address any further questions to my Mahter Magnifikat. Thank you and have a blessed day.*

Pahter Nuck looked up from the card. He scanned the massive figure—Sister Treesa's head crested up through the bent and pruned apple trees. "A little big, aren't you?"

Sister Treesa, unruffled, reached into her opposite sleeve. She pulled out another card and proffered it to the Pahter.

> *Hello,*
>
> *If you are reading this, you have expressed surprise at my size. I was born a prodigiously large woman, and because of this, I was never able to find a husband. I have committed myself to the seven heavens, which do not judge our bodies but rather our souls. I'm very sensitive about it. Please do not bring it up again.*
> *Thank you and have a blessed day.*

Pahter Nuck crumpled up the scrap of paper. "Do you have a *card*," he said, "to explain where the hell the Magnifikat is?"

The Sister shook her head, once.

"Isn't that interesting."

Instead, Sister Treesa pulled a crisply folded letter, sealed with the Magnifikat's own crest, from her sleeve. She handed it over.

Pahter Nuck, with a sour expression, broke the red wax seal and opened the letter.

Hello Nuck,

If you retain most of your prefrontal cortex, you will have noticed I am not actually present. I am on a buying trip. Buying what? Three guesses.

No, not that.

Not that either, you pervert. Get your mind out of the gutter.

Yes, Mechaneet. Ding ding ding. Lucky winner. Et cetera.

I'll be back soon. If not, I've probably been kidnapped by the Outlaw Queen. In that case, let chaos reign. Lay waste to the orchards. Loot the sakristy. What do I care? I'm dead.

Cordially,

Pahter Nuck pinched the bridge of his nose with two fingers. "And when is she expected back?"

Sister Treesa shrugged. She gestured for the men to take a seat on the bench and wait.

"No," said Pahter Nuck. He stepped up close to the Sister. "I have the *right* and the *duty* to investigate the premises."

Sister Treesa considered that. Then, she bowed, and gestured for everyone to come in.

Pecta was fourteen when Parat the Outlaw Queen captured her Kathedral ship. As soon as Pecta wrapped her mind around the concept that she was free, she secured a knife and sheared off all her shining black curls.

Like most Penitents, she had been created very beautiful. Pecta took steps to alleviate that. She allowed her eyebrows to grow unhindered, spreading like brushstrokes of ink across her brow. Pecta narrowed her eyes, and tipped her chin up when she faced someone, exposing the more severe lines of her neck and chin. She wore high collared shirts and soldier's pants, with so many pockets and loops and folds that it was impossible to discern the shape of her hips. It didn't make much of a difference, but it was something.

Pecta had not liked the Outlaw Queen in the beginning. Parat wore her hair like a macaw-bird, and subcutaneous lights gleamed blue in her cheeks and forehead. She tattooed a crown of indigo around her temples, studded with lights that glowed pink under her skin. The Queen out-talked everyone, leapt up on tables and challenged great hulking Blast Boys to duels, laughed loud and drank deep, then threw glasses to the ground to smash them. Pecta had considered her an idiot, a privileged pet of some Pahter, who had never really learned fear.

Pecta had learned fear. She had also learned to master it.

Penitents had internal armor, to survive the more brutal aspects of their existence. The armor allowed Pecta to survive a thousand blasts that shredded other Mechaneet to pieces. She rose through the mess that constituted the Revolution's rank system, and quickly proved herself the best of the warriors available: the most thorough, the most exacting, the most trustworthy. The Queen knew good optics when she saw it. She assigned Pecta to one high-profile extraction, and then another. Pecta's name became well-known among the Potentate—the frightening First Mate of the Queen, so beautiful, so fierce.

Parat trafficked in dreams and ideals: with them, she managed to capture the minds of a thousand, then two thousand, then ten thousand Mechaneet outlaws. She led a fleet of seventeen stolen ships, and terrorized the edges of the Potentate. Her newest dream was a partnership between Pecta and Parat.

"Don't you see?" said Parat, her arm around Pecta's shoulders. "Two halves of a whole. Together, we'll be unstoppable. You'll have to get tattoos, too. I'm thinking something dramatic: like stitches across your mouth." Parat drew a careless finger along the curve of Pecta's upper lip. "We'll have to make it pretty. Maybe tears down your cheeks. You know, the whole Penitent thing. Whatever makes you memorable."

Pecta didn't say a word. She suffered Parat's touch without a shudder. She'd learned this trick with the Pahters. They did not want a conversation. Neither did Parat. They wanted a canvas. Pecta folded herself away to a quiet place inside her own head, and waited.

Pecta's cell on the Magnifikat's transport was small. It was tiled all over in a parquet design, the ceiling a block of glowing light, the locked door sleek and red. Pecta lifted her one remaining hand up, and traced the lines of the tile on the wall with a finger. Without her augment, her right arm ended at a nub just before the elbow joint.

Pecta sat up against the wall, and spread her hand on its surface. She measured it with her handspan, then knocked the wall with her knuckle and pressed her ear against the surface. She jutted her lower jaw out, and scraped her teeth against it, to feel the thrum of the transport's inner workings.

Pecta had lived her entire life on an interstellar Kathedral ship. She knew intimately the differences between ceramic and silicate surfaces: she could tell within a finger-snap how well-traveled a corridor was, or the exact placement of an exhaust vent. Pecta knew how to pick up vibration from an interstellar ship's hollow walls, stuffed with processing equipment and coolant tubes.

Within seconds, Pecta knew the make of the transport ship. It was a bespoke model on the pattern of an old Sentinel design, small, but powerful, and brimming with security. The system in place required too much power to be anything but top of the line.

Fortunately, Pecta had been cleaning and refueling Sentinel transports since she was a child. She knew a few tricks.

Pecta ran her hand along the rim of the door, searching for the correct place: three handspans up from the floor on the left side. She balled her left hand into a fist, and smashed her knuckles into the ceramic. The tiles splintered, as if they had been struck by a sledgehammer. Her skin split and left a smear of blood on the tile. The designers overlooked a structural weakness in the ceramic. Humans never credited Mechaneet prisoners with any brains.

She reached in and with a nudge detached the inner uplink cable to the door lock. If she were right, the door would spring open once the system's explicit order to stay locked went offline.

Pecta was right. She squeezed out and flattened herself against the white wall of the corridor. She could see the helm of the ship, casting a beam of light down the corridor. The ship was tiny: two holding cells, a bunker down below for engine access, and a helm that barely had room for two pilot seats.

She turned, and with a rush of relief saw her arm, hanging from a hook on the wall outside her cell. Pecta could not understand why it hadn't been sold away already. A bespoke piece like hers could fetch a great price.

Parat had presented Pecta with the arm two weeks after the first Nowhere Battle. Pecta had used a needle-nosed transport to gut a Krusader battleship, but the explosion carved a chunk of flesh from Pecta's thigh, and tore her right arm off. Her armor was self-sealing: it pinched off the arteries and grew to cover the exposed bone within an hour. Pecta was never in any fatal danger. She killed more than two hundred Pahters in that maneuver.

Parat waited until Pecta could walk without a crutch, and then took her new protégé aside. Parat's face was alight with excitement. She unwrapped the arm for Pecta, and helped her strap the band across her chest. Pecta's face tautened in pain as the prosthetic shot a needle through her armor, into the flesh of her arm, and expanded out into a tree of artificial nerves, syncing up with her own system.

Pecta raised her new hand, a coppery, jointed creation. She twiddled her fingers, which came to wicked points.

"Try the new blaster." Parat hopped from foot to foot like a child.

Pecta bent her fingers back as far as they would go. The mechanism started to hum. Her digits folded backwards, and what used to be her palm started to shimmer with light.

Pecta leveled her gaze at Parat. "This is mine?" she said, her voice quiet and intent.

"Yes." Parat chucked her chin. "All yours."

"No one's going to take it away," Pecta clarified, her round face very serious.

Parat laughed her pirate's laugh. "I'd like to see them try. You've got me looking out for you, gorgeous—"

Parat froze when Pecta leveled the gun in her direction. Pecta advanced on her captain, backing her up against the wall. The humming muzzle of the gun pressed against Parat's chest.

"No tattoos," snarled Pecta. She was trembling, all over. "Do you understand?"

It took Parat a moment. When she finally understood, her eyes widened in horror. "Pecta," she said, her voice hushed. "Pecta, do you not want to be here?"

"You," said Pecta, her eyes wild, her teeth gritted together. "Never touch me again." She jammed the gun up against Parat's breastbone, painfully. "Yes, Captain?"

Tears filled Parat's eyes. She shook her head. "I didn't know," she managed, her throat constricted, her face reddening. "I swear—" she reached out a hand in pleading. "I swear I didn't know, Pecta. I had no idea. Why didn't you *tell* me?"

"Tell you what?" Pecta spat. "That I won't follow orders?"

"Those weren't *orders!*" Parat wept, both hands clutched around the gun pressed against her chest. "Pecta, I would *never—* seven *hells*, Pecta! What would make you think I would *ever—*"

Pecta stood there, gun extended. She waited, stone-faced, for Parat to stop talking.

Parat closed her mouth, tight. Her lips puckered where she bit them. She nodded once, in agreement.

Pecta powered down her arm. She turned and stalked from the room.

Parat found her, later, sitting at the dark mouth of an access hatch. The Kathedral core used massive metal cylinder shafts to cool and direct its heat to necessary places. Pecta faced the interior of a cylinder, her legs dangling down into nothing. If she fell, she would tumble directly down into the core.

Parat settled down next to Pecta. She was careful not to touch her.

"I was an experimental specimen," said Parat. Her lips tightened against an unspoken memory. "The Potentate needed test subjects for a lot of things. I was in isolation. Alone, in an antigravity cell. They would put me in stasis, then wake me up again." She shook her head. "Nothingness. All the time. My name's not Parat, Pecta." She gave a smile that was not really a smile. "Someone should know that.

"I don't remember the first name I was given. They kept me in that room until I couldn't remember. Nothing but dark. Nothing but walls. I screamed, I cried. I begged. Then, suddenly…" Parat tipped her head back, blindly. "They pulled me out of my box, and ran tests on me. I was fine. I hadn't lost muscle mass, my brain functions were normal. I just wasn't a *person* anymore. They put me in a uniform, and I scrubbed floors and walls. I was one of a unit of seventy. I followed orders. I looked just like everyone else."

Pecta pressed back a smile. Parat noticed, and raised her eyebrows. Pecta shook her head, and held up a hand in apology. "Everyone thinks," she said, "that you're an elite Church assassin gone rogue—one of a kind, an expensive and secret experiment gone wrong—"

Once Parat got the joke, she grinned too, and covered her mouth with her hand. "Oh, yes," she said, through her fingers. "I am a masterpiece."

Silence stretched out between them.

"I think you should spend some time recruiting," said Parat finally. "I've reassigned you. Espoid. It's a shit smear of a planet." She looked over at Pecta. "But it's not here."

Parat stood up and left.

Pecta remained sitting, facing out into the bone-cold darkness of the cylinder. She contemplated the thought of touching earth.

Pecta fit her shoulder into the joist of her arm. She felt the needle slide into place, and begin to regrow the artificial nerve stems. Her control would be piecemeal for a couple of hours, and it would hurt like hell. But she had a weapon now.

She stole her way up through the corridor. It was only twenty paces to the helm of the ship: a rounded curve of viewport and control holograms, scrolling out in blues and whites. The light silhouetted the Magnifikat, who sat in the pilot's seat, reaching out to correct a line of instruction with one slender finger.

Pecta waited until she was a handspan away from Mahter, standing directly behind her chair. Then she primed her arm. "Freeze," she said, through her teeth. "Don't make a move, human."

Mahter Magnifikat slowly raised her free hand into the air. She swiveled in her chair. Her face, all cheekbones and eyebrows, expressed something closer to mild surprise than fear. She had unpinned her veil, and twisted and wrapped it clumsily into a knot on the top of her head, a length of the sheer red cloth protruding out from the side like a tongue.

Mahter's mouth was full of bread. She held a bun in one hand, toasted brown on the outside and soft and white on the inside. There was a crumb on her lip.

Pecta's eyes snapped to the bread without her intent.

Mahter, after a long moment of silence, her face illuminated by Pecta's humming blaster, extended the piece of bread out to Pecta.

Pecta had been a refugee in the camps on Espoid long enough to know that you ate whenever and however you could. She took the bun from Mahter, and sat down in the co-pilot's chair and ate. It was excellent.

The Magnifikat settled back against her seat. She was still all angles and posture; she still looked like her body had been molded around a steel pike. "I assume if you wanted to splatter my brains across the wall," she said finally, "you'd already have done it."

Pecta spared her a glare, her mouth full of bread. "There's still time."

The wall of the cell pulsed with white light, and Mahter frowned. She looked up at the barrel of the gun Pecta had trained on her. "May I take this?" Mahter inquired.

Pecta nodded her permission. Mahter pressed her hand to the surface. "Hash—I mean, *Treesa?*" Mahter touched a finger to a hidden earpiece, and turned away in her chair. "Yes. Oh, he's there now? Wonderful."

A beat of silence, then Mahter again said "No. You can't kill him." Another beat of silence, then Mahter grinned for real, leaning back in her chair, folding her bony arms across her chest. "Because it would involve a lot of paperwork, and probably some mopping, too.

"Now, listen to me." Mahter's voice became intent. "Pull rank, and privilege. You work for a Magnifikat, and he's only a Pahter. Stall him, misdirect him. See if you can keep him abovedecks. Play dumb. For heavens' sake, don't unveil." Silence, for a moment. "Oh, he'd like to talk?" Mahter rolled her eyes at Pecta, as though they were old friends. "I would enjoy nothing more. Put him on, please."

Pecta reached out with her hand, and touched the speaker option on the call. A voice rippled out through the helm. "Mahter Magnifikat." Pahter Nuck's voice was clipped and sour. "So unfortunate that we missed each other. What's your excuse, if you don't mind me asking?"

Mahter eyed the gun that Pecta had trained on her chest. "I'm busy. And what have you turned up so far, Pahter?"

"Your orchards are sub-par. The Church's regulations on fruit tree husbandry set forth by the Third Korov Council clearly state that trees must be more than six feet apart and spaced in rows. You have grown yours in a hexagonal grid."

Mahter grinned and leaned back in her seat. "Oh, goodness. Oh, seven heavens. Whatever shall I do for penance? Wear a veil and take orders from bureaucrats?"

"Is there something more important than turning up for your inspection?"

"I rather thought that was implied by my absence, yes."

"What have you been doing?"

"Before this conversation?"

"Yes."

"I was pacing the length of my ship, wondering about the Church's official position on apple tree husbandry."

"Clever. If you're not careful, I'm going to get offended."

"Oh, what are you going to do, *forgive* me?" Mahter hung up on him with a *click*. She let out a sigh, massaging her temples. She looked up at Pecta. "Old friend," she said, as if in explanation.

"Anyway." Magnifikat turned back to her screen. "You were saying."

"I was saying I could kill you now." Pecta's voice was cold and calm.

"Noted."

"Are you planning to kill *me*?"

Mahter raised her slender eyebrows. "Why would I do that?" She grinned. "And, I would ask, under the circumstances: *how*? No, this is not all a villainous preamble before I reveal that the floor opens up to a roiling pit of sharks. This is just me dealing with several shovelfuls of shit piled on at the same time."

Pecta opened her mouth to ask for specifics. However, at that moment, the ship's wall console flared a bright and urgent red. The Magnifikat was silhouetted, briefly, by the glare. She frowned, and tapped the input screen for visuals.

The white of the wall dissolved into an intricate geometry of color. Reds and greens and golds in triangles etched out a picture of a man with a shepherd's crook and two sheep. It took the two of them a minute to understand what they were looking at.

"And another shovelful," said Mahter. "A Kathedral port," She pinched the bridge of her nose, and parsed out the situation in her mind, spreading the fingers of her other hand as she figured. "If they knew me, they would have hailed. So…"

"It's the Outlaw Queen," said Pecta, gazing up at the screen.

"What spectacularly bad timing," said the Magnifikat, calmly.

The ship on the screen drew closer, revealing hundreds of black weapons ports. Kathedrals were built for defense. Their sheer size accommodated a reactor that could manufacture and replenish fire as it shot. The glass ports glowed from the forge of the reactor within.

Mahter turned to issue an order to Pecta. An ear-shattering explosion drowned out her words.

Pecta was protected by the armor built into her anatomy: flexible shatterproof plates covering her vitals, armoring shoulders and elbows and knees. She knocked her head against the door, drawing blood from her temple, but that was all.

Mahter, meanwhile, hurtled backward, past the door, her veil spiraling through the air. She hit the far wall with a *thwack*, and crumpled to the ground.

The helm throbbed with red light. Someone was hacking into the ship for unauthorized entry. The transport's door opened up with a warning alarm.

A round woman with a bright quiff of pink hair and too many guns rounded the corner into the cell with a skid, accompanied by a platoon of soldiers. She registered Pecta, and froze. She removed her helmet, her golden eyes wide with disbelief. "Pecta?"

Pecta powered down her weapon. "Parat."

Parat approached her. Without thinking, she tackled Pecta in a hug that was half-embrace, half-inspection for wounds, mistreatment, damage. Then, Parat remembered herself, and stepped back. "Pecta," she said, a shade too loudly. "We found you just in time." She cast a contemptuous look at Mahter, unconscious on the floor. "Looks like Mahter Magnifikat's about to get a taste of her own medicine."

Pecta accepted a hand up. She pointed to the cell in the back. "Nine more," she said to the other soldiers. "And Parat? We can't kill her."

"Oh, I know," said Parat, stepping up to the Magnifikat, eyes hungry. She nudged Mahter with her boot, her eyes livid and hungry. "Not yet."

Pahter Nuck stood in the middle of an orchard in lavish bloom, his expression sour. He folded his arms.

He and the other Pahters had been given a tour of the orchards, the gardens, the fruit gardens, the vegetable gardens, and the canal system, which cunningly made sure that no room, planted row, or tree was more than a few feet away from water. Nuck had already tripped into a canal twice. The Sisters had shown him to the Magnifikat's traditional throne, set up on a raised dais to survey the garden. The throne was wicked in its construction, jet black and cut from polished stone. Behind the throne stood the infamous black doors, the image of which circulated the Potentate at regular intervals.

Then, the Sisters took them back behind the doors.

The first corridor led into an appropriately grim operating theater. A stark metal table stood on a concrete floor with a drain at the center, floodlights illuminating the restraints for arms and legs.

The table was big enough for a Blast Boy, and blood painted the floor. It was all very sinister. Quite picturesque.

Then, the Sisters had led him back beyond the operating room into a hallway lined with barred cells. A chorus of wailing greeted him, hands extending out through the bars in supplication.

Nuck knew what suffering looked like. The Aktuates had picked him up at the age of eleven, off what remained of a disease-ravaged colony on Gasrat. He knew what hunger looked like; he knew the smell of fear.

"These Mechaneet seem rather—" Pahter Nuck paused to inspect a Sentinel model with four arms and a metal plate patching its skull, "well-fed."

The other Pahters were horror-struck. Nuck heard Pal and Lukis murmuring prayers as they passed through the dark hallway. "Seven heavens have mercy on these poor creatures," said Pal, to no one in particular. Nuck rolled his eyes.

"Oh, sweet Pahter," gasped a filth-covered and very handsome Penitent, on the ground, his hair gathered up in an entirely too well-kempt knot of dreadlocks. He reached through the bars and gripped Nuck's ankle in one hand. "Please, have mercy on me. Take me home with you. I'll scrub your latrine. I'll dance like a little fucking wind-up toy."

Sister Treesa let out a snort. The Penitent shot a look up at her that was closer to mischief than fear. He certainly had marks from punishment, striped along the skin on his back, but they were old. This Penitent had not been beaten to cleanse the sins of someone else in a long time.

Sister Treesa pointed, and the Penitent crawled back to the wall on his hands and knees.

Pahter Nuck rearranged his sutayn. "I'd like to see the lower levels, please."

Sister Treesa guided him to the end of the corridor. The wails of the Penitents followed them like well-rehearsed music. A red door, illuminated by twin amber lamps set into the wall, stood before them. Sister Treesa gestured towards the lock on the door, then signaled helplessness by spreading her massive palms.

"You can't open it?"

She nodded.

Pahter Nuck stepped up to Sister Treesa. "Take me belowdecks," he said, calmly. "Or I will send a report to the Glorifikarum themselves, detailing your disobedience and recommending a complete—What in seven *hells* do you think you're doing?"

Sister Treesa had put out a massive gloved palm, to halt him. She reached her other hand up to her ear. When Pahter Nuck tried to complain, Treesa placed her hand on his face, engulfing it and muffling his words. Treesa stood stock still, her finger on her ear. She turned back to her Sisters. She raised one hand and made a series of wordless gestures to the other members of her order.

They immediately turned from the locked doorway, and escorted the Pahters out of the corridor. The Sisters parked the

Pahters on benches in the orchard, and one of them disappeared inside the kitchens. She returned with a tray of tea and cups, and served the Pahters as they sat.

The Sisters made their way to a wall, and with the push of a hidden brick, slid back the wall to reveal a staggering weapons locker, full to bursting with blasters, stun grenades, and shock launchers.

The Sisters armed themselves quickly. They slotted a seemingly endless stream of gun after gun beneath the smooth red façade of their veils.

Nuck and the other Pahters watched, agape, as they passed by once more, on their way to the secondary port. When Nuck tried to block their passage, Sister Treesa amiably picked him up by his shoulders off the ground and put him aside.

They disappeared around a corner, toward the auxiliary ship ports, and were gone.

Pahter Nuck and his retinue stood abandoned at the center of the beautiful garden.

Nuck gritted his teeth. He turned to the other Pahters. "Wait here," he instructed.

"What exactly are you planning to do, Nuck?" said Magnapahter Lukis.

Nuck did not respond. He crossed to the weapons wall, and selected a blaster that had been left behind. He primed it, and stalked back to the doors.

He made his way down the corridors. The prisoners started up their wailing again, though they quieted when he did not even slow in his stride.

It only took four blasts to blow the door off its hinges.

Once the debris cleared, and Nuck's eyes adjusted, he strode through.

When Parat the Outlaw Queen boarded the Kathedral ship, she had made short work of the Pahters on board. The Mechaneet outlaws had rounded up all the Pahters and pushed them down into a cylinder hole, into the reactor. The Pahters burnt up as if they'd never existed. A fitting end, explained Parat to her people. That's what the Pahters did to Mechaneet that had outlived their usefulness.

The Dominikat, however—the ruler of all the Pahters, part priest, part captain, second only to the Glorifikarum—with him, she had taken her time.

Pecta knew what it was like to have someone *take their time* with her. For that reason, and that reason only, Pecta decided to take up guard outside the Mahter's cell.

The cell itself was a cube of bars, directly outside the helm of the ship. Parat, walking past to confer with the pilots, absorbed Pecta's self-imposed post in front of the cell. They met gazes. Pecta did not lower hers.

Mechaneet in bands dropped by to stare at the Magnifikat. They shouted insults, but with Pecta there, glaring at them, they did not dare to come too close.

The Magnifikat was broken and bleeding in a dozen places from the blast. Her eye was badly swollen. She held herself as if her ribs were broken. Mahter sat up against the wall, her skirts forming a neat crinolined circle about her person. She had unfurled her veil from around her head, and let it fall down over her body once more.

Mahter's one good eye glimmered with a hint of merriment, not least because Pecta herself stood hands clasped behind her back, her gaze firmly fixed on a point in space. She had not moved in the last two hours.

"So," Mahter said, her words easy. "When are you planning on killing me?"

Pecta's amber eyes snapped to meet the Magnifikat's. She stared Mahter down, studying her intently. She looked away again. "We're not," she said.

"Trading me, then." Mahter considered that, tapping her fingers together. "Smart. Who came up with that?"

Pecta didn't respond.

Mahter looked her over, her eyes much more careful than her words. "Do you know," she said finally, "what the real difference is between a human and a Mechaneet?"

Pecta raised her eyebrows at Mahter. The Magnifikat's gaze was mild.

Pecta pointed to her amber eyes. Mahter shook her head. "Cosmetic difference," she said. "Done intentionally, to differentiate you."

103

Pecta turned her back, and tugged down her collar to display the external vertebrae that many Penitents had—a line of steely dots, poking up through the flesh.

Mahter shook her head. "Not that either."

Pecta shrugged.

"Nothing," said Mahter, almost wearily. "There's no difference at all. Mechaneet are humans."

Pecta took that in, silently.

The Mahter tipped her head back against the wall. "Intergalactic domination is tricky," she said. "It requires much moral compromise. Mechaneet are a convenient way to circumvent many of the rules of the church. The morality advertised by the holy writings, when parsed out by the soulless, really only extends to other humans. You're not *people*, that's the main thing," said Mahter Magnifikat. "And within that premise is an infinity of possibility." Even Pecta could not ignore the hatred in the Magnifikat's voice.

Pecta waited a moment before she spoke. "I used to get tortured on this ship," she said, glaring at the wall before her. "Every day."

Mahter opened her mouth to speak. She thought better of it, after she saw Pecta's expression. She inclined her head once. She waited.

"And now I live here." Pecta struggled with the words, opening her mouth and then closing them again. "It's better. But I am still—" She couldn't say it.

"Hunted," said Mahter, watching Pecta carefully.

Pecta shot her one livid glare, her lips pressed together.

"You could leave."

"There's nowhere else to go."

Mahter opened her mouth to say something, just before an explosion rocked the ship. Pecta stumbled forward, then righted herself on the post of Mahter's bed. "Hull breach!" she roared, into her earpiece. "Get the squads out to the perimeter, now!"

Parat barreled around the corner, strapping on her armor as she grabbed Pecta's earpiece and slotted it into her own ear, listening to the chaotic maelstrom of voices. She cursed, her eyes wide. She looked up at Mahter. "They're here for you," she snarled.

"Oh, goodness," said the Mahter. She folded her hands across her belly. "I'll do my best not to swoon."

Parat strapped on her breastplate. "Pecta, stay here," she ordered. "Do *not* let her escape. She's our only bargaining chip."

Pecta pulled out her viewing screen and looked at the scene of the battle. A ship had broken the outer armor along the nave of the Kathedral, betting on the ship's automatic reflex to absorb and seal off projectiles to minimize the risk of life support breach. The ship had taken the bait, allowing the nose of the sleek battleship to poke through into the nave itself.

A red-cloaked figure popped open a hatch, and tumbled out. Dozens of outlaws descended on the figure, and it came up blazing, a blaster in either hand, tumbling the outlaws to the walls. More and more of them came, faceless, relentless red Sisters, armed to mow down anyone in their path.

Pecta frowned at the screen, then up at Mahter again.

The Magnifikat inquired *what?* with her eyebrows.

Pecta considered the woman before her for a long moment. When she finally spoke, her voice was quiet and intent. "The Unseen Kompanion," she said. "What does that mean?"

Mahter spared her a thin blade of a smile. She looked up at the ceiling of her cage. "It's an astrological term," she said, perhaps the first words to come out of her mouth not touched with sarcasm. She rested her head back against the bars. "An ancient one. A very long time ago, back on Earth, astronomers could only detect some planets by their gravitational effect on their star." Mahter framed an imaginary scene with her hands. "An invisible planet that tugs the orbit of its sun off-balance. A very small thing—too small to be detected—changing the path of something huge and horrifying."

Pecta considered that for a long moment. She narrowed her eyes at the Magnifikat.

Then, she primed her arm, and took off at a sprint.

Pecta thundered down the steps of the sanctuary to enter the fray in the nave. She shot several concussive blasts to either side of a Sister, knocking her crossways and finally onto her back. Pecta straddled her, and took hold of the scarlet veil. She flipped out the blade in her thumb, and tore the fabric apart.

A pair of amber eyes blazed up at her, enraged. A Blast Boy, horribly disfigured, his nose missing, glared up at Pecta. He hefted her up like a sack of cotton, and rolled over so he pinned her to the ground. "Where is the Magnifikat?" he yelled. "What did you do with her?"

Pecta met Parat's eyes from across the nave. Parat looked round-eyed at the unveiled Blast Boy, then cast her gaze over the other veiled Sisters, fighting their way through the Mechaneet outlaws of the Kathedral.

"Cease fire!" Parat roared, struggling up. "Everyone, stop, now! *Cease fire!*"

"It's mostly a question of location, after the initial purchase or drop-off," said Mahter. She sat propped up against the steps leading up to the wrecked sanctuary, one arm clasped tight around her broken ribs. "There are a few sympathetic communities, and some Mechaneet can pass for human, with a little surgery. Not Blast Boys or Mine Boys, but we do what we can. Some of the more—visible—Mechaneet stay at the Abbey and become Sisters. It is certainly not a requirement, but it is a life."

Pecta stood against the abandoned altar, silent, as she came to terms with the world gone upside down for the second time in her life. "Are all Abbeys like yours?" she said.

"No," said Mahter, using her knuckle to wipe a smear of blood from her lip. "No. We are unfortunately unique."

* * *

The moment that Pecta had realized the truth, she dashed back to Mahter Magnifikat's cell and dragged her back to the nave, to show her people—her *Mechaneet*—that she was alive.

"For heaven's sakes, everyone calm down." Mahter had said, leaning heavily on Pecta as she stood on the raised platform of the sanctuary. "I'm fine."

Sister Treesa—also known as Hash—looked up at her. His eyes widened. He stormed up to his bloody-faced Mahter, dwarfing her by two feet. He hefted her up with both arms. "Take me to your medical bay," he growled to Pecta. "*Now!*"

"My," said Mahter, dryly, wedged against his chest. "How swashbuckling of you, Hash." She patted his shoulder. "I'm afraid your coping mechanism is going to have to wait. I imagine that Pahter Nuck is poking his nose around the Abbey at the moment?"

Hash confirmed it. Mahter let out a quiet stream of very impious and imaginative profanities. "Then," she said, tapping Hash's arm so that he would put her down. "We are going to have to improvise."

"Three circumstances converged to create the mess we're in now." Mahter continued to explain. Hash had convinced her to sit on the steps of the apse, a blanket wrapped around her shoulders, while he crouched before her and tended to her bleeding face. "One," she said, "the famous First Mate of the Rebellion, the outlaw Pecta, apparently in what, deep cover in a runaway camp?"

"Recruiting," said Parat, lips numb.

"Recruiting, thank you, Your Majesty—was captured by a slaver and put to auction. Naturally, we had to try to get you to safety. Second, the good Pahter Nuck of the Aktuates decided to come and conduct an inspection at precisely the wrong time. And third, Parat the Outlaw Queen spotted my transport in her territory and decided, quite sensibly, to take advantage. Now we are deep in the shit," said the Mahter. "At least knee-deep, if not higher. We might be able to slog our way out of it, but it will not be pleasant."

Mahter looked around at the Mechaneet surrounding her, and snapped her fingers in impatience. "Well, I can't be expected to come up with *every* idea, can I? Pitches, ladies and gentlemen. Now, please."

"I have a plan," said Pecta, straight-backed and fiercely intent. "But it is dangerous."

"And I have a major concussion, so I'll probably think it's brilliant." said Mahter, wavering where she stood. "Let's hear it."

"But what in seven heavens do you mean, Pahter?" quavered Magnapahter Lukis.

"I mean exactly what I say," growled Nuck. He jabbed a finger at the black doors. "There is *nothing* down there. There is one operating room—ostensibly for show—And then past that—rooms. Hallways and hallways of rooms. Not even cells. The doors don't lock." The rooms were well-furnished and warm. "Then, below that, there's a working floor packed with *fake identification cards* in the process of being pieced together—"

"Pahter," ventured Pal. "This is unbelievable."

"I assure you," said Nuck. "It's all true. As soon as we get in contact with the Glorifikarum, I will obtain permission for you to enter the inner sanctum as well, and witness it for yourselves."

They were spared from further contemplation by the unmistakable *whoompf* of a ship docking at the port. They looked up at Pahter Nuck, who appeared just as confused as they were.

"That sounded like a Kathedral," said Pal, craning his head to look out the doorway.

"Impossible," said Nuck. "They would have hailed us."

The doors to the foyer thumped under the force of a mighty blow, then burst open, and a stream of red-veiled Sisters barreled through, wrestling with filthy Mechaneet outlaws, bearing them to the ground and shocking them into submission. Parat the Outlaw Queen herself was there, unhelmeted for full effect, spitting curses at the Sisters as one hauled her up and another bound her arms behind her back.

And then a figure, in the sheerest veil possible, her headdress a pristine crescent atop her head, sailed through the doorway, a struggling, spitting Penitent held captive under her arm.

As the Pahters watched, Mahter drew a glinting knife from her belt, grabbed the Penitent by her hair, and slit her throat in a flash of silver. Red blood streamed down her shirt. Her eyes rolled back and she went slack in the Magnifikat's arms.

"*Pecta! No!*" screamed Parat. "*You'll pay for this!*"

Mahter dropped the knife on the ground. "No, Outlaw Queen," she said, loudly. "It is *you* who will pay, I think."

She turned to the Pahters, ranged out in front of her empty throne, frozen with shock.

"Ah, gentlemen." Mahter let the bloody Mechaneet fall to the ground. "Forgive my delay."

She signaled to her Sisters, who began to drag away the unmoving Mechaneet, and wrangle the struggling Parat up towards the black doors.

The Pahters parted to allow Mahter to pass among them. "Although I am extremely busy," said Mahter, using her veil to wipe a splatter of blood from her face. "I feel I must give you an explanation.

"I know that the rumors of experiments being conducted with new breeds of Mechaneet have been flying around the Potentate. Well, they're true. We have been." She waved a dismissive hand at Parat the Outlaw Queen as a Sister hauled her past the Pahters. "But this gutter trash is not the result."

Mahter stalked her way over to Pahter Nuck. She reached out and she took his chin, studying his every feature, carefully. It was a show of attention, a piece of theater. "Under the direct orders of the Glorifikarum himself," she said, her voice low and grim. "My humble order created a new kind of Mechaneet soldier, which could be hidden in plain sight." She stood directly before Pahter Nuck. "As one of us."

Pahter Nuck understood after a long, silent moment. He let out a long hiss of breath and shook his head. "You have to be joking." He sounded more annoyed than anything else.

"Did he explore the dungeons, gentlemen?" Mahter said, her face imperious, her hands behind her back. "Did he come back up and insist that this Abbey is a wicked place and must be shut down—presumably because we are inept, and not, of course, because Pahter Nuck might secretly object to experimentation on his fellow Mechaneet—"

Pahter Nuck turned back to face his brothers. "Mahter is manipulating you."

"I am a Magnifikat, Pahter." Mahter tipped her chin up, majestic in her offense. "Is your Glorifikarum capable of error to the degree of appointing someone unworthy to my post?"

"That's not what I meant and you know it."

"Did he say," said the Magnifikat, resplendent in her veil, her hands pale against the scarlet cloth. "That there is no research occurring on this ship?" She spared Pahter Nuck a look of deep contempt. "Does that claim not on its own inspire suspicion? If the Glorifikarum appointed the Sisters of the Unseen Kompanion to make use of these—" she indicated the bloody corpse of Pecta, sprawled across the floor, "vermin, then who is this Pahter to investigate and proclaim otherwise?"

And then Mahter steepled her fingers against her chest, and took a step back, lifting her chin. "But clearly my arguments are not necessary," she said, carefully. Her gaze flicked up to Magnapahter

Lukis. "Because it occurs to me that a gang of wise and subtle Pahters, in wishing to trap a traitor, might simply go along under that traitor's *leadership*—" Mahter indicated her sarcasm with a flip of her hand, "and, under the pretense of helping him *investigate,* instead deliver him directly to the prison he deserves."

A long beat of silence. Mahter Magnifikat pinned the old Pahter with her eyes.

Pahter Bendikt was the first to take the bait. "I knew from the beginning," he said, stepping forward. He turned around, his back to Mahter Magnifikat. He raised a trembling finger up to Nuck. "Mechaneet traitor. Now you can't escape."

"I am not a Mechaneet," said Nuck calmly, his arms crossed.

"Exactly," quavered the elderly Magnapahter Lukis, turning away from the Magnifikat, as he leaned on his gilded cane, his eyes fervid with conviction. "*Exactly what a Mechaneet would say.*"

After that, it was a mess of denunciations. The Pahters formed a ragged line, ranged out, shouting over one another, standing before the Magnifikat's throne as if in a line of defense.

Nuck stood alone before all of them. He did not speak to the Pahters. He raised a glare to the Magnifikat on her dais. "Very clever," he said to her, over their heads.

Behind the line of the Pahterhood, slumped back on her throne, Mahter Magnifikat, aimed one finger at the man before her. She brought the hammer of her thumb down, slowly, as she grinned.

Pahter Nuck's mouth pressed into a white line. He didn't say a word.

Mahter held two fingers up over her shoulder. Two veiled Sisters swept forward. They towered over the Pahters, and in response to a silent command, they grabbed Pahter Nuck, and escorted him towards the passage. He didn't struggle.

The Sisters also yanked up a protesting Parat and company by their bindings, and marched them off down the passageway. They disappeared into the darkness. An infernal glow cast their shadows long and flickering on the opposite wall, before they too faded and vanished.

(Another Sister, with less fanfare, crouched down and with infinite tenderness picked up the slaughtered first mate Pecta in her arms. The Sister carried her away, quietly, in the opposite direction.)

The Pahterhood, once Nuck had disappeared, fell into an uneasy silence.

"Is it true?" Pahter Naytan stepped forward. "Are there...are there really Mechaneet that look like us?"

"In short?" Mahter Magnifikat turned in her chair, and immediately clutched her ribcage, her whole face tautening with silent pain. She clutched the armrests with both hands. She looked down on her audience. "Yes. May I ask a question of my own?"

Magnapahter Lukis nodded once, and the Magnifikat clasped her hands together under her chin, and leaned forward, her eyes glittering. "Did you allow Pahter Nuck unfettered access to my lower decks?"

"I'm afraid so, Magnifikat."

Mahter hissed out a breath of disappointment, turning her head to the side. "Then there is very little chance," she said, "that he did not sabotage our security in some way. We do not have time to search the premises, gentlemen—I have six thousand pirates to imprison. I must ask that you all—precious Pahters—leave at once, to keep yourselves safe, and bring the news to the Glorifikarum. If we suffer attack or prison break, they *must* know."

"Yes." Magnapahter Lukis immediately turned to leave. "That would be the honorable thing to do."

"Of course it would. But," Magnifikat held up one hand. It was testament to the weight of her presence that even the Magnapahter stopped and turned back to her, as if she were one of the Glorifikarum. "I must tell you now." Mahter gripped the arms of her chair and leaned forward. "As you have seen for yourself, our entire Church—the entire *Potentate*—faces an untold danger. We have ways of learning who is human and what is Mechaneet—" In those words, Mahter managed to imply grimness and terror. "But the reach of the Sisterhood is not long. Until we can muster up our forces," she said, clasping her hands together. "Remember. They could be your brothers. They could be your friends. They could have replaced your Pahters and Magnapahters. They may go after the Glorifikarum."

"God help us all." Magnapahter Lukis' voice was hushed with horror.

The Magnifikat raised a hand: in warning, in blessing. "Go," she said. "Now, my sons. For the love of God, *before it's too late.*"

The Pahters scurried for the port dock.

Mahter Magnifikat hauled herself up and off her throne. She made her way over to one of the vaulted glass panels, clinging to the wall along the way, and peered through it. The beacons on the Pahters' gold-paneled transport flared, their thrusters blooming with blue light.

Once the ship had plucked away from the Abbey, and flicked off into the star-speckled distance, Mahter let out a long, slow breath, through her teeth. She turned around and leaned against the glass panel. She chuckled weakly to herself, pushing her headdress up. A lock of grey hair fell over her eyes. *"Before it's too late,"* she repeated, grinning. She looked up at a Sister, who had followed her to the window. "Not too much?"

The Sister threw back her veil to reveal Hash's broad, homely face, his eyes amber and narrow with worry. He helped Mahter stand up again with one hand, and gestured out the window with the other. "Apparently not."

She grinned up at her oldest friend her eyes full of wicked merriment. "Not bad for an old bat with blood loss and a concussion."

Hash rolled his eyes. "Yes," he informed his Magnifikat. "You are astounding."

"That I am." Mahter's eyes closed, her face pale as the apple blossoms. "Now is when you catch me, Hash," she instructed. Hash obeyed, snatching her up before she staggered to the floor.

Pecta's throat ached, and her lips were terribly dry. She let out a groan, her eyes closed. Somebody clasped her hand tightly, with rough fingers. "Pecta." Hash's voice was quiet, and gentle. "Pecta. Can you hear me?"

"Let her sleep, Hash." Mahter's voice was too sharp not to belie anxiety.

Pecta reluctantly slit one eye open. She put out a hand to stop the light, streaming in from a bronze-edged glass window. Hash moved his massive frame between Pecta and the window, blotting out the light entirely.

Pecta spent a good minute or so coughing. A wet cloth touched her lips.

"Parat," she managed, finally. Her voice was like gravel.

"Gone." Hash's voice was matter-of-fact. "She took the ship and left as soon as she could. The Potentate is in a state of panic. Everyone thinks the Outlaw ship escaped from Mahter Magnifikat's Abbey with thousands of freed Mechaneet prisoners. They couldn't let an opportunity like that pass."

Mahter's veil usually fastened under her chin, suspending her face owlishly in pleats of red. Now, she let it fall to either side, draping over her black-clad shoulders, like the headdress of a bride. Mahter held a cup of some clear liquid in one hand, a krystallite bottle in the other. She winked at Pecta, and leveled a dramatic gaze out the window. "No. Damn you," she muttered into her glass. "You may have won this round, but I'll get you yet. Et cetera."

Pecta's gaze found the Magnifikat's face. One of the old woman's eyes was swollen and violet, the other bright as a silver blade. "Is that alcohol?" Pecta's voice cracked, her throat aching terribly.

"Yes," said Mahter, raising the glass and swirling the clear liquid. "We make it here. It's the only thing about this place that's terrible."

Pecta found herself pressing back a smile. She reached out and took the bottle from Mahter. She used two hands, to be sure she wouldn't drop it. She took a swig, then grimaced. "I think," she said, "you're right, Mahter."

"I'm always right." Mahter reached out to take it back, but Hash was too quick, snatching the bottle from between them. Hash pushed Mahter back into her chair with one firm hand. "Stop drinking with a concussion," he said.

Mahter's eyes narrowed. "Let me die how I want to, sir."

"You're not allowed to die, Magnifikat."

"And why not?"

"Because when you do," said Hash, turning away and replacing the krystallite bottle on the shelf, "they'll make you a saynt."

"Oh, fuck me," said the holiest woman in the galaxy.

"That's right. Well—" Mahter leveled her gaze at Pecta, her slate eyes grim, "I suppose now I have to live forever."

Hash, his arms full of stripped bedding, stopped at the window. He let out a *chuff* of laughter, and looked back at his Magnifikat. He tapped the pane with his thumb. "Someone is unhappy."

Mahter and Pecta craned their heads to look.

Nuck sat on one of the stone benches that lined the circular garden. His arms were crossed. Nuck still wore his sutayn, black against the white stone. The blooming apple trees half-obscured his face in a spill of pink and gold. He sat in the dappled light, his face sour. Seven small, smooth white cups sat clustered on the bench next to his right leg.

As the three of them watched, a Sister approached him with a steaming kettle of tea, and offered him a cup. Nuck turned his head away. She placed the porcelain cup down on the bench, next to the others, and turned sideways to move past him on the narrow path, kettle swinging in one hand.

Mahter clucked with her tongue. "I'm going to send him somewhere really, really beautiful." She looked up at Hash, her face aglow with mischief.

Hash, being Hash, shook his head, his eyes full of pity. "All he wants is a universe that makes sense," he said.

"Stupid," said Pecta—or, rather, Pecta heard herself say. She contemplated the white and pink blossoms on the trees, through

119

the bronze-framed window. She turned her head, and saw Mahter Magnifikat studying her.

"Yes," said Mahter. "Idiotic." She lifted one hand, swathed in white bandages, to point out the window. "The trees blooming. The waterways running. Senseless. Absurd." Mahter waited a beat. "You can stay here," she said to Pecta. "For as long as you like. You know that, right?"

Pecta considered that for a moment. She nodded, once. "I won't wear a veil." She leveled her gaze at the Magnifikat.

"No one will ever ask you to." Mahter's gaze was even and calm. She ran her thumb around the rim of her glass.

Pecta searched the Magnifikat's face for lies. Satisfied, she settled back into her rumpled sheets. Pecta turned onto her side, and trained her gaze on the window, looking out into a vast old pleasure garden of greens and silvers.

She didn't close her eyes for a long while.

Only once Pecta had truly fallen asleep did Mahter Magnifikat tear her gaze from the back of Pecta's head. She looked up at Hash. He raised his eyebrows.

"I'll go to bed," said Mahter. "I promise, Hash. I'd like to stay up for her. A while longer."

Hash considered it, then took his leave. The door closed after him with a soft *click*.

Mahter tipped her head to the side, her jawline sharp and winnowed to a point. She took a contemplative swallow, then held the glass in both hands, her index fingers steepled over the rim. She was all scarlet in the light from the window.

Ungodly Hour

Ashlee Kilpatrick

It was not the creaky sound of the interworking rusted gears beneath the decorative walls that brought tension to his muscles. It was not the mechanical spiders creeping around the study that caused his heart to beat faster. It was not the unsettling smell of blood in the air that made him want to hold his breath. He would rather fear any of those things—or everything in all the world—than the very woman sitting in the study room before him.

The infamous leader of the Heretics gang.

Madam Aranea.

The Madam Aranea.

She sat on a velvet crimson sofa with her arms spread out on the back of it and her long legs crossed. An odd-looking brown wooden cane with a curved golden head rested besides her on the edge of the sofa. Her long, raven curls streamed down her broad shoulders and over her high-collar black top. One of the mechanical spider's legs pinched at her light brown skin with its sharp tips as it crawled up her hand. She pursed together her pale red-painted lips before she flashed her teeth, beaming an elated grin towards him. As if she was about to sink her teeth deep into him and eat him alive.

She had to be the most beautiful yet terrifying creature his eyes had to ever gaze upon. But he knew she was more than what she appeared to be. Mr. Darling gave him thorough instructions about what to do in his meeting with Madam Aranea. He advised him to be tremendously cautious about the words that left his mouth and the actions he took.

She is a godless woman with immeasurable power.

A danger.

A heretic.

She could kill you in the blink of an eye if she wanted to. Don't be stupid.

"Come in, Mr. Bowden," Madam Aranea beckoned in a low, sultry voice. "I've been expecting you for quite some time now."

George Bowden half-heartedly bowed, pressing a white-gloved hand over his heart for a mere second, ensuring that his revolver was well hidden underneath his navy dress coat. Slicking his blond hair back, he closed the steel door behind himself and concealed his nervousness as best as he could.

But as he walked over to her, footsteps creaking on the wooden floor, his whole body wanted to shake. To tremble. His hands began to feel clammy beneath his gloves.

Distress had him in a tight chokehold that he desperately needed to escape from. He thought he was completely prepared to face Madam Aranea today, though he was truly not sure anymore. He didn't know why he was invited to her manor so suddenly, but he prayed it had nothing to do with his personal plans. She couldn't have discovered that he was behind the new conflict between her gang and Mr. Darling's gang.

Could she?

"G-Good evening, Madam Aranea. It is truly a, uh, surprise that you wanted to see me like this," George stuttered, extending his hand out to her. He smiled, but not too hard.

Or too wide.

Charming.

He needed to come off charming, like Mr. Darling instructed him to.

"Well, what can I say? I thought it would be such a pleasure to finally meet one of Mr. Darling's best men in the flesh. His new Rook." Madam Aranea said, slightly tilting her head to the side. "It's not easy for some to make it to second-in-command for Mr. Darling," she shook his hand with a firm handshake, looking so welcoming.

But that did not help calm him down at all. It only made things worse.

"As it is a pleasure of being in the company of yours, m-madam." George hesitated, retaining his smile.

Right before he let go of her hand, the mechanical spider that was sitting on her hand swiftly crawled onto his hand. He gritted his teeth tight as the spider went up his arm, then made its way down his chest and to his leg. His attempt of hiding his utter disgust failed, seeing how Madam Aranea threw her head back and laughed heartily.

No, cackled.

She cackled loud and wicked.

Like a mad woman.

"They're harmless, Mr. Bowden," she cooed. "They may act a lot like the real thing but there isn't anything to fear."

She clasped her hands together in her lap. Then she flashed her teeth again, beaming that same elated grin like before.

"Trust me," she said.

George nodded, even though he could never do that in all seriousness. Trusting Madam Aranea was claimed to be one of the worst choices to make in Irongate, somewhere between selling one's soul to the void and eating anything from that old abandoned greenhouse by the docks.

"I...I apologize for my reaction, madam." George took a seat in the armchair across from her and cleared his throat. "I'm not used to such peculiar machines as yours."

She responded with an amused hum. "My precious little creations can be very foreign to most, so I believe I can understand."

His gaze briefly slipped past her shoulder, to the several mechanical spiders climbing up and down on the wall, feeling his stomach twist into a large knot. He hated robotic machines more than spiders to be honest. He couldn't stand the concept of them. They were vile contraptions and, sadly, everywhere he looked in Irongate.

"So tell me, George Bowden," Madam Aranea began before stretching her hand out and carefully examining her sharp, red fingernails. "You're not originally from Irongate, are you?"

"No, ma'am." George answered, then wanting to punch himself the second he uttered that word.

Ma'am.

Madam Aranea glared softly at him, balling her hand into a closed fist, causing him to grab the edges of the chair to keep his hands still and hinder his inner panic. Mr. Darling warned him about calling her "ma'am". She considered it a sign of disrespect.

Keep it together, George.

"I'm from Crowrath," he added as nervous laughter slipped his lips. He needed to be calm. Charming. But he didn't feel like he was being either of those things in that moment.

Keep it together.

She tossed her hair over her shoulder, eyeing up and down at his appearance. "Crowrath? That's a long way down from here." She arched a thick eyebrow. "That's rather interesting."

"It's not really," George muttered, trying so hard not to grimace. He loathed thinking about his life back in his hometown. A miserable little town on the ground. The life he had there was a poor and ugly one. He was a nobody—nothing. He was never returning to that life, of that he was certain.

Not this time.

Madam Aranea grinned at him. It appeared kind but—in his bones—he felt something colder. It was like a dagger driving deep into his lungs instead of a warm-hearted gesture.

She casually waved her hand through the air. "Of course, it's interesting. Irongate doesn't often get a lot of new grounders. Mr. Darling and I used to be grounders, in fact." She snorted, grabbing her cane and starting to get up on her feet.

"You and Mr. Darling were?" asked George, leaning forward in his seat.

"Surprising, I know. And to think we still are close to this very day too. But he doesn't enjoy telling others that we grew up together as kids." She yawned, covering her mouth. "I believe it might have *something* to do with the fact I murdered his whole family with my bare hands when we were eleven."

George held his breath, digging his nails into the edges of the chair. She was getting personal with him. Crime lords don't share information about their lives in formal meetings. It was… inappropriate. He didn't expect something like this to happen. This was not a good sign.

"Shocked? I don't understand why you are, Mr. Bowden. I'm sure Mr. Darling and everyone else in this town have spoken plenty of ill things about me." She stood with both hands resting on the head of her cane.

"I've only heard the things Mr. Darling has said," he lied. He had heard all the rumors and stories about the horrible Madam Aranea within the first month he started working for Mr. Darling. Some say that she was a godless horror that walks among Irongate. Known for her acts of corrupting the beautiful women in the town and murdering wealthy aristocrats.

She was a godless woman with immeasurable power.

A danger.

A heretic.

"He speaks nothing but good will."

This time she did laugh, a dry laugh, which caused him to believe he was going to die in this very chair.

"Mr. Darling is always full of it. Charming through his little lying teeth. Such a bore. And yet they never considered him to be the monster he is," Madam Aranea said, walking towards him with cane in hand and a pronounced limp.

"But for myself, I have no trouble of showing my true colors. I know damn well enough of who and what I am. Accepting myself is what got me where I am now."

"As a crime lord, madam?"

"No, as a *queen*," she said as the corners of her lips rose.

Absentmindedly, George snickered at her.

He snickered at her.

He had the audacity to snicker at her. He shouldn't have. He had no right.

But he did it.

Madam Aranea shot a glare at him. "You think that's funny?" Her fingers flexed around her cane's golden handle and then unclenched. He opened his mouth but his tongue had turned to lead. He sunk himself deep into the armchair, lowering his head.

She scowled and then her face suddenly changed with a haunting smirk overtaking her features as she continued. "I don't see what's so funny about what I just said. Nor do I find someone who's so cowardly and witless to attempt to cause a conflict between Mr. Darling and me to be funny either."

"I—I don't under—understand what you're going on about?" George countered, shifting his gaze between the floor and her face.

"You don't understand? Well, let's see what's not to understand about what I am going on about. Shall we?" Madam Aranea tilted her head to the side as her eyes flickered to glossy and black instead of a sharp brown. "You, a pathetic little man, thinking that it would be possible for you to get away with such unforgivable crimes amongst your own people and mine. Manslaughter, theft, slander. And all for what? To cause a gang war between two of the most powerful crime lords in Irongate? How...childish."

George hurriedly slid his hand in his dress coat to draw out his revolver, but Madam Aranea was quicker than him. She unsheathed the blade hidden in her cane and slashed off his gliding hand in one quick slice, sending it crashing to floor, right between his feet.

"Though it's a pity, Mr. Bowden, that we had to meet at such an ungodly hour. But you needed to learn that you could play the underworld game all you want. But do not forget that I own this game more than you ever will." She ignored his frantic screams and stabbed him right in the heart, twisting the blade as hard she could. She pulled her blade out of his heart, beaming at the now lifeless body in her armchair.

"I am the queen of this criminal underworld. And I refuse to become a mere pawn in my own damn game." Madam Aranea shifted most of her weight on her right leg as she seized his white glove, wiping his blood off from her blade. She wanted to kill him right when he entered the study. Slit his throat clean for all the stupidity he created. But she always did have that terrible habit of toying with her targets instead of being so straightforward. It was more fun drawing them into a false sense of security and allowing them to act unafraid of her presence.

Madam Aranea stared at George's open and still blue eyes, feeling greatly satisfied about her handiwork. Another spineless man attempting to take her throne. Another spineless man taken by her blade. It was sad how often this happened to her. People always wanted to take the very things she had fought to get. Since she was a little girl, power was all she wanted. Because she had been Narcisa Bílá. A scrawny grounder nobody from the Miorita country, struggling to do better. She did not live that life anymore. Never again did she want to be Narcisa Bílá.

As she slid her blade back into the cane, the study's steel door opened and footsteps creaked towards her. She sucked in a quick breath as she placed some weight onto the cane. A mechanical spider came down on a wired web, landing on top of her shoulder. Madam Aranea made a humming sound as she smiled at the spider.

"Don't worry, my little one." She laughed. "Death is only the beginning of his punishment."

Empty Spaces
Chloe Leach

Veris knew hour by hour how the town came awake. The rhythm of the pre-dawn was important to someone who couldn't afford to get caught with her hand in the wrong pocket. It was like watching a clock being wound up, slowly beginning to tick away the same pattern it was bound to perform every day. In those very, very early mornings, no one cared about keeping track of anything but themselves and the things they were trying to do. That made it easy to watch.

There were few exceptions during her morning vigilance, and even those she had memorized by season. A celebration in the winter and one in the summer, the hustle and fuss of the harvest for those who had farms in the flat pastures to the south, the days when merchant caravans swept back into town after having kept their distance from the steep paths during the months of snow. The festivals held every year to celebrate heroes long dead and, aside from the aforementioned pomp and circumstance, long forgotten.

Today, however, she did not wait for the world to wake under her watchful gaze. Today, Veris had different plans.

The truth of the castle was that it was much more impressive from outside. It must have been exceptionally impressive today, of all days, and Tetha was sure that if she saw it from the edge of the city, towering and bedecked in colors, she would have been just as awed as anyone. That knowledge had never granted her much fondness of the place, however. She loved the town well enough, and the ocean stretching out beyond it. She loved the hard dirt road connecting her with all of it. She didn't love the cold, though.

Heavy blankets pulled up nearly over her head, Tetha curled her toes and her whole body into the heat of her bed as she listened to the muffled noises of her father talking downstairs. Someone would come to get her before long—they should have already, really, but there was a sense of wanting to give the young lady room to breathe this morning. Not because the festival was anything dreadful in general, or anything dreadful to Tetha in particular, but because it was her first year taking on this role, and it seemed the right thing to do.

Pressed against the northern edge of the castle as it was, with only two narrow windows, her room didn't let in much light during the very early, very cold dawn hours, but what did get through was enough to make out her costume. Tetha peered at it suspiciously. There was a pair of plain breeches, a light blouse, and a simple jacket to go with it, which had been added at her particular request. The whole show was meant to be simple, unrecognizable, aside from the mask.

To Tetha, it seemed a thing alive. She had seen other people in masks before, for the festival, she'd seen her father wear many different ones through the years. She'd never had one for herself, though. There were plenty of children that did, because it was fun and their parents let them, or because they'd managed to nick one from a booth, but it meant something much different for Tetha to show her face. It was a display of youth, a promise that she was still learning her role. Only the proper ruler wore a mask. Only the proper ruler needed to hide their face and lose themself in the crowd.

The designs changed every year, and for every person, though not many had their masks custom made. Tetha's had delicate green scaling, which crawled past empty eye sockets and over imagined cheekbones. She'd had to sit for hours while the leather base was molded to her face and the designs sketched out, coming back for repeated sittings to ensure that the pattern was flattering and the shape hadn't deformed. That was weeks ago. Now it hung across from her, completed to the finest detail, fins of soft green cloth with delicate metal ribbing splayed out from its blank imitation of her own face.

The knock at the door came as no surprise, and Tetha quickly drew herself up, still clutching her blankets. "I'm already awake, Liffy, I'll be out in a minute."

Liffy came in anyway, unperturbed, a bustle of auburn hair and freckles. She still had a pile of dirty plates balanced in one hand, presumably from breakfast, as she eyed Tetha suspiciously.

"Do you need help getting ready this morning? It's quite a day you've got ahead."

"I'm fine, Lif. I don't think pants have changed all that much since the last time I wore them."

Clucking in a dismissal so casual that Tetha wondered why she even tried, Liffy set the plates down with a small clatter and started to examine the outfit. She fussed with the sleeves of the blouse, muttering a bit about them being too long, but quickly discarded the illusion of being interested in anything else but the mask. With a care she only showed when it was required of her, Liffy ran her fingers along the top, held the frills out in their full display. There was a moment of quiet as Tetha watched her examine them.

"The green will look horrid on you, honestly, it's not your best color. The crafting is lovely though. And a dragon, of course. Everyone loves to be a dragon their first year."

Tetha shrugged, focusing instead on her search for the boots she'd kicked under the bed the night before. She did not want her feet touching anything remotely resembling stone this morning. One boot was right at the edge, but the other had fallen over, and Tetha was bent over the side of her bed trying to reach it when she heard Liffy sigh.

"I'm proud of you, I hope you know. Your father is too, even if he doesn't show it. This may seem all showiness and tradition to you now, but it means something. To us and to the town. It's a bit of a shame I won't be able to see your face when you realize it."

Face still hidden, body still hanging half over the edge, Tetha grabbed the other boot she'd been searching for, taking a moment to dig her fingers into the fur lining. Then she pulled herself up, a bit off balance, but quickly steadying herself and giving Liffy a smile. The woman was still turned away from Tetha though, still fiddling with the mask, now admiring the delicate golden gilding on the biggest scales at the edge of the face.

Slipping both boots on, Tetha walked over, untangling one blanket from the pile to keep wrapped around her shoulders. Up close, the scales resolved themselves more clearly into treated metal, coaxed into a bright, bluish green, each given a slight curve and fitted together against the wood. Tetha grabbed the pants, holding them against her chest as she glared at Liffy.

"That's all very good, and I do know today is important, but I'm still getting changed by myself. Is breakfast laid out?"

Taking the hint, Liffy assented, moving a step back, and then another, before going over to picked up the discarded dishes. "I made sure there was still enough left out for you. It's probably started to go cold though."

Tetha nodded, still standing by where the rest of her outfit hung, still holding the pants. "That's fine. I'll be ready soon."

The celebration took place at the top of town, which was inconvenient for Veris, but hardly impossible to navigate. She fished out her mask as she made her way up, slipping along parallel to the main street of town. The alleyways were cleaner than usual, but still coated with the lingering smell of trash and rot. It was a smell and presence that Veris was accustomed to, as she pressed herself against a cool brick wall and peered out. The day had already begun, much earlier than any other day. The echos of tired, easily excitable children bounced down the road off of sleepy buildings, followed by the half-hearted voices of adults trying to keep them quiet. It didn't matter much. Within the hour, everything would be loud, and no one could really complain about being woken up early on a festival day.

Veris grinned, her first such allowance of the day, and tied her mask so it hung loosely around her neck. It was one of the cheap ones that merchants made in the dozens, not a real artisan's mask. She wasn't even sure what it was supposed to be. A bird of some sort, judging by the rough feather patterns gouged into the wood. She'd fancied it a hawk or an owl at a glance. If everything went well, she wouldn't even have to put it on, which was good, because it had a rough patch against the left cheekbone that hadn't been sanded down properly, and it narrowed her vision down by half at least, if not more. It was a backup plan amidst backup plans, and it thumped reassuringly against her chest as she ducked back into the dim light and began to jog deeper into the maze of alleys.

The path Veris had found, poking around abandoned buildings almost half a year ago, didn't lead directly to the inside of the castle. Worse than that, the entrance wasn't even tucked away somewhere useful and quiet. The only reason she'd found it at all was because Rut had taken it upon himself to try and start up old feuds. It had rankled her pride to have to back off of the territory she'd so long considered her own, but he had numbers, and a renewed bitterness, and Veris knew that waiting out his anger was easier than confronting it head on. So she'd retreated, headed to the empty streets at the top of town, tried to lay low for a while. Which was why she'd found the path. Or, as she thought of it, The Path.

Veris was fairly sure it was meant to be an escape route, once. There were still torches affixed at both ends, bolted into the walls, and the structure was well built enough that it didn't seem in any great risk of collapsing, at least as far as she could tell. It must have been old though, and seemed completely forgotten. No one was worrying as much about fleeing from the castle these days, apparently.

The entrance into town was tucked away in the dusty fireplace of a boarded-up dress shop. This had been one of the properly fancy places, once. It was easy enough to tell by location alone. The inside was empty, all peeling wallpaper and cobwebs, and a bit bigger than the buildings Veris usually found to hide out in. She was half-convinced that something magical had led her there. The hand of fate itself had caused her to kick down the boards on one of the back windows, had pulled her along like a child's toy through the dirt and grime, to an ashy, long forgotten fireplace. Fate had struck a match and started the flame, and fate had helped her kick out the embers in just the right way so that her boot hit the brittle false back and tore through it like paper.

There were plenty of crooks like Rut that would say there was no such thing as fate, just skill and the whims of chance. A real thief knew better.

* * *

By the time the morning bell sounded, Tetha was dressed and had at least managed to make a passing attempt at breakfast. The food wasn't nearly as cold at Liffy had threatened, and it was as good as ever, simple and filling.

It was hard to focus on eating though. Tetha hadn't been nervous the night before, or any of the nights leading up to the festival. She hadn't expected to feel so uneasy. She'd attended often enough, it wasn't as though the steps were unfamiliar. Any kid old enough to look forward to fall and the end of the season could recite the speeches. It wasn't like she'd forget any of that. But it was still her first real time participating, and there was that mask.

It sat on the table as Tetha pushed her eggs into a soggy pile, trying not to make eye contact with the space where eyes should be. She was trying to figure out if she'd had a secret lifelong fear of masks that she'd somehow forgotten about, the way that people sometimes did, just cutting out a worry so entirely that it no longer existed for them. She didn't think that was the case, though.

No one was waiting for her outside in the courtyard by the time she made her way down, so Tetha did her best to be small and out of the way. She saw Liffy darting out of a door now and then, but didn't catch her eye, and no one else paid any more mind than they ever did. There were several carts lined up at the front gate, loaded with all the things too particular to prepare in town. When she snuck up to them and peered down the road, Tetha could see that two more carts had already left and were making their winding, rickety way down.

Eventually, recognizing the few attendants she knew always accompanied her father for trips like this, Tetha made her way over to the carriage she was supposed to travel in. She nodded at Hester and Briston, the attendants, who nodded in return, one stepping to the side and opening the door to the carriage. Her father's hands were just visible, covered in the familiar black leather of his gloves, folded quietly on his lap. Tetha watched the hands as she stepped up, helped by Briston. They moved slightly, unfolded, then folded again as her father nodded at her, making a soft noise of acknowledgement that sounded as though it had been swallowed halfway out.

Sitting across from him, Tetha arranged her own hands to mirror his and looked out the window, watching Liffy stride across the courtyard to harangue one of the workers who had dropped one of the brightly colored banners that were to be strung up around town. She could just make out Liffy's voice, but the wind carried away enough of the words that there was no meaning to it. Just a sense of nervous energy and focus.

Only once everything else was sorted and everyone else gone did Hester and Briston step into the carriage themselves, giving the front wall a knock once they were settled. The carriage started forward with a rickety burst of movement, the landscape suddenly jostling by. Most of the fog had burnt off, though there was still a persistent, damp cold on the breeze. It smelled like rain, and Tetha slumped down into her coat against the chill, sticking her hands into her pockets. Across from her, she watched her father adjust the cuffs of one of his gloves.

Preparations were underway by the time Veris reached the festival square. Most of the thin crowd was comprised of staff from the castle, making themselves busy laying out food and decorations, and checking that the booths were sturdy and clean. The central ones would soon be filled with the most well respected of the local cooks, who offered their own creations to the larger spread of food—sugary pastries, mostly, and a smaller selection of anything warm, savory, and usually covered in some kind of bread. Warmth was key, and Veris watched the larger dishes being laid out with no small sense of longing. Normally, she looked forward to both the variety and quantity of free feasting offered. But no one was around yet to eat, and by the time the festival had started in earnest, she planned to be long gone.

In the meantime, she tucked herself into the shadows of the roof, digging in her position amidst the half-collapsed chimney. The empty shop, the actually important building, was a few houses down, but she had wanted to make sure that things were underway before trying to slip off.

Flicking a bug off her boot, Veris adjusted her position to take the pressure off of one of her legs. More carts were coming down from the castle now, forming a semicircle around the stage as the first of the morning wanderers that Veris had passed earlier began to make their way up. The kids had flocked together at the front of the group, lead by younger siblings who clutched at the hands of the older siblings left with the task of accompanying them. A small gaggle of girls branched off from the main group, excitedly examining the table of food from a distance. Parents and young families followed, and lone, quiet figures, and some clutching well-bundled infants that occasionally let out complaints even Veris could hear. No sign of Rut and his goons yet, and Veris was sure she'd know them even with the masks.

It had always seemed pointless, the fuss about masks and disguises, as if not knowing a name or a face meant that you couldn't know who someone was. They were all the same crowds, following all the same steps. The details were interchangeable. It made the scene feel stale, even in the crisp air. This wasn't a small town, from what Veris knew of the world. It wasn't a quaint seaside village, or an isolated handful of cottages in the distant hills. With its tightly packed mess of old buildings and narrow streets, eventually spreading out into the wider farmland outside the city, it was just small enough to get bored of. Smaller still, she figured, for someone like her.

Running her hands down her closely shaven head, Veris pulled up her hood, sinking further into the roof and lying back to look at the sky. She was completely out of sight that way, unless someone was on some other roof, and even then only from one direction. It would be fun to watch more, but it would mean risking being spotted. She'd been on the roof many times, but never when a festival was happening, and never when it mattered so much to be unseen. So she contented herself to listen, as the people poured in and the sounds of work and preparation melted into sounds of conversation, laughter, and hum of excitement. A few people were shouting out last minute sales of masks and other costume fineries, hats and scarves to keep warm and complement the day.

It was easy to tell when the real nobility finally arrived by the sudden hush that fell over the crowd. Loud in the new quiet was the sound of a carriage pulling up, and horses being settled, the sounds of servants and attendants and workers, the only sort still moving in the moment of collective waiting. Then the sound of a door, of careful feet and faint murmuring.

The sky was a hesitant blue overhead, though it faded to grey at the horizon, darker still in the parts hung with rainclouds. The sun was clear and sharp though, not as warm as it had been a month ago, but as bright. Veris watched two hawks circle each other through the clearness, each chasing the other in lazy loops.

There was talking. Somewhat faint, and muffled further by the heavy fabric of the hood pressed against her ears as she lay flat. The typical introductions, Lord such and such and his daughter, Lady so and so. A remembrance of summer. A remembrance of warmth. A remembrance of the fall and growing winter they would face together, a singular people. Acknowledgements, respects paid, a special flourish about light or fire or standing firm. Then the real speech, the same one every year, louder but even harder to make out, as the entire crowd joined in. Veris followed the words more by memory than by sound.

"By the fire we shall stand together," she mouthed into the cool air, licking her chapped lips as the town took a breath, "through the darkness we stand firm."

Tetha stepped off the stage after the recitation, hands still a bit shaky. She hadn't tripped over any of the phrases, and as far as she could tell the words had been loud and clear. At least passably so. Her father was still sitting on the makeshift throne, where he would stay for the rest of the day, Hester and Briston positioned beside him. It was a boring job, staying behind on the stage. She hadn't even been able to go get food the years before, each time having to work up the nerve to ask one of the attendants to go get her some. Everyone was allowed short breaks, of course, to stand up and stretch and take care of other business, but it was still a long, dreary wait as Tetha remembered it. As uneasy as she was to take on her new role this year, she was more than happy to hand the old one off.

As she stepped a bit away from the crowd, she could see a handful of kids already with masks on, running up to one of the tables and eyeing its contents. They were all birds, mostly dull colors, brown and tan cut through with patterns in black and white. Painted, not actual feathers. As Tetha watched them, she felt a hand on her shoulder, and turned to find Liffy next to her, the dragon mask in her other hand. It was shinier out in the sunlight, more visibly metallic. Still keeping a hold on her shoulder, squeezing slightly, Liffy handed off the mask and began to guide Tetha behind the stage. The two stood together in a second of silence, removed from the growing energy of the crowd.

"Make sure no one can see you when you put the mask on. It's bad luck."

"I know, Lif."

"And you can take a moment, if you want. Everyone will be wandering, you should be able to slip into the crowd at any time."

"All right."

Liffy squeezed again, a bit firmer this time, and then turned to leave, pulling her own mask out from the bag perpetually slung over one shoulder. Even with the mask, it was easy enough to tell that Liffy was Liffy. And Tetha was sure her own elaborately decorated creation would stick out, even if there were plenty of other specially made masks nearly as fine.

Tetha took a few steps forward, marveling at how quickly the sound died down once she was behind the heavy wooden structure of the stage. With a glance over her shoulder, it was clear she wasn't properly covered yet. A few people shot her furtive glances, turning away quickly if she made eye contact, and Tetha herself turned quickly back around and hurried towards the center of the empty area, until she was alone.

Stopping, she let one hand rest on the back of the stage, tracing the grain of the wood as she tried to make out the muffled voice that she thought might be her father's, as he sat on the other side. The support beams carved out the space in front of her into clean geometry, and beyond that were the cold, quiet structures of the long abandoned parts of town.

Holding the mask up nearly to her face, Tetha took a deep breath and held it, counting down from ten like Liffy did whenever she was cross. She could hear the thunk of an arrow hitting home, which meant at least a few people had started the games. Mostly though it was conversation, and the sound of plates and cups and dishes being moved and shuffled, picked up and set back down again.

Eyes closed, she let out her breath and raised the mask to her face, feeling leather against her cheeks and nose, the new pressure almost like an itch. Holding it in place, she began to tie the ribbons behind her head, and as she did she looked up again, and paused. A few buildings away from her, dressed all in black, someone was frozen mid-step, one hand on the door in front of them. Their hood was up, and the rest of their face was covered by a cheap wooden mask.

Tetha stood with her hands above her in a tangle of half-knotted ribbon, eyes locked with the glimmer of someone else's eyes behind the mask. Then she drew back a quick breath to say something, blinked, and they were gone.

Back pressed against the closed door, Veris did her best to steady herself and focus on moving forward. She had been much closer to being caught than before, she knew how to stay calm under pressure. It was a matter of shoving everything else to the side and narrowing down on a single point; a plan, a need, a gap to cross. She just needed to keep going. Being seen wasn't the same as being followed, and if she moved quickly, any attempt at following would be a tricky thing.

It still took a few deep breaths before she was able to push off from the door and make her way somewhat shakily through the empty rooms to the tunnel. Setting her bag on the ground, Veris quickly and carefully began to move the bricks she'd stacked in front of the hole. She chewed her lip as she worked, slipping the mask down back around her neck and weighing the benefits of trying to brick the entrance back up behind herself. It would take time, and it wouldn't be a very neat job. On the other hand, if she was followed, it might be the extra time that kept her trail clear.

Veris finished clearing the space and dropped her bag down the hole, starting at the sudden sound of laughter outside. She quickly squirmed in after it, legs kicking into open space before finding purchase on the inner wall, and then on the ground. The broken panel laid on the ground next her bag, where she had discarded it when first exploring. The laughter outside faded back into the distant, vague sounds of revelry it had sprung from.

Wrinkling her nose, Veris stood on the tips of her toes and peered back out of the hole hanging now in the wall just slightly above eye level. There was no sign of anyone else inside, no sounds of a door opening or other feet crossing the floor. The building was empty.

With a huff, she gathered up her bag and replaced the half-shattered panel, slotting it into place with a click. It was better than nothing, and she wasn't going to worry about it more than that. The long walk up the tunnel would be simple and boring, but after that she'd have to be sharp. Even a mostly empty castle was still guarded by someone.

It was two shallow turns and the beginning of an upward slope before Veris heard the faint scuffling and the thud somewhere behind her, and once again froze in place. As if that would make any difference here. She started to speed up, paused again, turned, and took a half-step back. It might not be a good idea to continue forward blindly. It might be better to confront whoever was following her. Maybe she could wait for the person to catch up and try to catch them by surprise. There were a few loose rocks in the tunnel, heavy enough to knock someone out. It was pitch black in here, it would be easy to get the upper hand.

"Hello?"

Tetha pushed herself onto her feet, brushing dirt from her pants and the back of her shirt, and called out again into the darkness.

"Is someone else in here?"

The light from the room above only lasted a few feet before fading into syrupy black, just enough that Tetha could see the size and shape of the place, the heavy packed dirt walls and the first of what she imagined would be a series of support beams leading forward. She could just make out an unlit torch on the wall in front of her, and took a brief second to make a futile search of her pockets, in case there happened to be a match in one of them.

There was no response from further in. No sign of life. From outside she could still make out the sounds of the festival. She should go back, though Tetha was also fairly sure that part of her mask had crunched against a wall on her awkward landing. The left fin, which had gracefully fanned out from her peripheral vision, now seemed to take a sharp bend and disappear. It was either bent or completely broken, and the rest of her was covered in dirt. It would be a bit harder to blend in with the crowds now, at the very least.

Biting down absently on her thumbnail, Tetha took a few steps into the darkness. There really was nothing to see, and she turned around after blinking a few times, turned her head back to capture the light floating down behind her. To remind herself it was there. Staring back at the opening again, Tetha felt a surge of guilt. This wasn't what she was supposed to be doing. This wasn't where she was supposed to be. She had no way of knowing if someone else was down here, and whether that person might not mean her well.

She closed her eyes, and turned back around.

As if in protest, the whole world began to buck.

Veris was inching closer to the mouth of the tunnel when the earthquake began. It wasn't the first she'd ever felt, though the silence around her was almost disorienting. Usually there was noise, people in shock, the sound of precious fragile things falling. The only sound here was quiet, and low, almost like a sigh.

Then a shout, from ahead. The same voice as before. Dropping the rock she'd been holding, Veris crept more quickly forward, as her footing started to shake more severely. Loose dirt and rocks rattled and slid down the tunnel, louder than the other sounds. For a moment, Veris lost balance, her foot slipping off of unsteady ground, sending her down hard on one knee. Another shout up ahead, and panic began to rise in full, because what if someone else noticed, what if whoever was in here got hurt, what if—

Veris collided with warmth, the heat and softness of another body, tripping her and sending her tumbling forward. The other person shouted again, in surprise but with a twinge of something Veris recognized as pain. She laid unmoving, half on top of the interloper, as the shaking finally stopped. Even then, she didn't move. Her hands stung from where they had hit ground, and her knee was scraped and sore.

There was no light to see by, but the form under her groaned, and shifted. Veris focused on breathing, then began to retract, to gather herself up. She pushed off into a crouch, and began fumbling around in her bag, glaring into the blank while she fished through what now seemed like so much clutter.

"Are you all right?" The voice was shaky, like it had been crying, or upset. Unsteady. When Veris didn't answer, after a moment, they spoke again. "Hello?"

With a huff, Veris found what she was looking for, pulling out her tin of matches and slipping a fingernail under the latch to flip it open, careful not to spill any. She hadn't been planning on needing light, knowing the tunnel's path well enough without it, and there weren't many in the tin—only four or five, if she remembered correctly. Matches weren't exactly precious, but they took more effort to get than food, being not so readily displayed, and she didn't like to use them without reason.

Pulling out one of the matches, Veris dragged it quickly across her leg, striking a quavering flame. She held it out, examining the other person, who leaned away from the sudden light. She had a mask on, a nice one, though the decorations were broken in several spots. Her clothes were plain, as was the tradition for the festival, but even though they were dirty and torn in places, they looked new, with no frayed edges or soft, worn patches. She looked young, maybe around Veris' age, though it was harder to tell because of the mask. Even with the mask, however, it was easy enough to see that she was scared.

"Who are you?" The girl was trying to keep her voice steady now, with moderate success. She was studying Veris in return, eyes darting from face to clothing to bag to face, and Veris briefly cursed herself when she realized her own mask was still hanging loosely at her neck.

The flame started to lick down the match, and Veris grimaced at the heat, transferring it into her other hand and holding it as low as she could. The other girl watched the movement, and after a brief second turned to point behind herself.

"There was a torch back there, I think, on the wall to the right. I don't think it's far."

Veris nodded, and shook the match out, pressing her fingers into the dirt to cool them off. Then she stood, carefully stepping around the girl, putting one hand on the wall as she made her way forward.

There was some light ahead. Not as much as there should have been. Just enough to make out the collapsed pieces of brick and stone spilling down through the opening above. Veris poked at a few of them hesitantly. It was hard to tell how much debris might be stacked up outside. If it was just the area around the entrance that had collapsed, she could dig her way out eventually. If the entire house had crumpled around them, it would be harder, if not impossible.

The sound of movement and scuffling behind her reminded Veris to look for the torch, which was still attached to the wall as it had ever been. Another match, a flare of bright light, and then the wider, blunter light of the torch, and Veris dropped another piece of charred wood to the ground. The mess in front of her was profound. The tunnel itself didn't seem like it had buckled, just the entryway, the rigid dirt structure littered with a pool of junk. Veris sighed, and grabbed the torch. All this meant was that she didn't have an escape route. Forward was still good. It had to be.

* * *

After a few attempts to stand, Tetha finally managed to ease herself up, leaning heavily on the wall. She could see light somewhere in front of her, getting brighter as she watched. The torch, presumably.

Her ankle throbbed. She didn't want to look at it, but it felt hot and uncomfortable, and refused to support weight. At least there was light now.

The other girl rounded the bend, torch held in front of her, and immediately caught Tetha's eye, shaking her head.

"I know it's collapsed, if that's what you mean."

The girl just frowned, shrugged her shoulders, and continued forward, pushing past Tetha.

"Where are you going?"

She turned, and shrugged again, then narrowed her eyes, examining Tetha the same way she had before. Tetha just gestured at her ankle.

"I think I twisted it trying to crawl out, when the earthquake started." Tetha paused for a moment, then added, "Can you talk?"

The girl sighed, and shook her head.

"Will you help me? I don't think I can get very far on my own."

She didn't move, still staring, dark eyes focused beyond Tetha. Then she took a few steps forward, switching the torch to her other hand so she could loop her arm around Tetha's waist. Tetha leaned into her, slowly transferring her weight until they came to an awkward sort of balance. Then she nodded.

They set off awkwardly at first, and Tetha bit back questions as they walked. It felt like it was probably kind of rude, to ask someone questions they had no way to answer. Still, as grateful as she was to be moving forward, it was uncomfortable not to know what they were moving towards, or why the girl was here in the first place. She'd known about the tunnel, she'd been sneaking away into it. Did she know where it led? She had to.

The grip around Tetha's waist was firm, a bit more than it needed to be, four thin fingers pressing her into the stride. The path was heading steadily up now, and after a few more curves had more or less straightened out. There was nothing to mark their progress, nothing outside the bubble of light.

"I guess you can't tell me your name, can you?"

No response. Tetha grit her teeth and focused on walking.

When they reached the end of the tunnel, Veris paused, taking a moment to balance the torch into an empty mount on the wall. The exit on this end was a trapdoor, and unless the entire castle had collapsed, it would be clear. The girl would figure out where they were, though. If she hadn't guessed already. Even if she had been someone ramshackle and common, this would be trouble. Her mask meant money though, her bearing meant money, her soft hands and long, carefully tied up hair meant money.

It had been a long time since she had wished for an easy way to communicate. On her own, it didn't matter much—it didn't take words to steal, and it certainly didn't take words to piss people off. How was she supposed to work her way out of this, though? By giving up, maybe, running off and disappearing back into some cramped alleyway. Or leaving the girl behind.

Veris had liked to think she was better than that, though.

The girl was still quiet. She hadn't spoken again, and was eyeing the door above their heads, carefully not making eye contact.

Sighing, Veris walked both of them over to the back wall of the tunnel, ducking down and slipping the girl's arm off her shoulder. With a strained smile Veris lowered her to the ground, eyeing the ankle as the bottom leg of the girl's cuff slipped up. It was swollen and red, but didn't seem like anything worse than a bad landing. The puffy skin looked odd and unhappy above the dirt-stained cream of the girl's socks.

Giving another brief smile and a thumbs-up, Veris turned back to the trap door, straining up to the tips of her toes as she grabbed at the chain above her head. One swing for it, another, and then she caught the metal ring, stepping back as she pulled down, just in case anything fell out from above when it opened. The structure creaked and protested for a long second, swollen wood whining against the frame before its inevitable surrender. The door swung open, a rope tumbling down after it. There hadn't been one the first time Veris had found the door, but she'd put one in once she made it up, so that it would be easier next time. Tugging on the rope, Veris made sure it was still firmly anchored, then turned back to the other girl.

She had slipped off one of her shoes and was examining her ankle, head turned down but eyes still following Veris. Eyeing the rope, she started to struggle with the shoe, trying to tug her heel back into it and wincing as she did.

"Do I have to climb that?"

Veris did her best to keep her expression even, a task she'd never found easy.

"Right." The girl discarded her attempts at putting the shoe back on, holding it loosely in one hand as she struggled to her feet. "I guess that's a stupid question."

It was, but Veris just shrugged. Maybe she should just leave the girl down here. Someone would probably find her eventually. Or maybe Veris could leave a note behind after she had found enough treasures. Thanks for the stuff, also there's some rich dragon stuffed down below the crypts.

Limping forward, moving more gently than she had to, the girl reached the rope, testing it just as Veris had. She still had her mask on, it was still hard to read her expression underneath, so Veris watched her hands instead, the fingers that curled and uncurled, not trusting their grip.

With a click of her tongue, Veris gently pushed the girl a few steps back, reaching for the rope. It was coarse and cheaply made, enough to hold her weight and not much beyond that. Veris tossed her bag up first, then scampered up after it with little trouble, pulling herself onto the cold stone floor. Then she reached a hand down through the door, gesturing at the girl to grab hold and continue up.

Hesitantly, she grabbed the rope. Curl, uncurl, grasp again. Reaching up, she grabbed at Veris' wrist. Before she could let go again, Veris pulled.

"This is below the castle, isn't it?"

Tetha didn't exactly recognize it. She'd never had a particular interest in exploring the catacombs under her home. She knew of their existence and their general layout, and little beyond that. The heavy, delicately inscribed stone slabs were hard to misjudge, however.

Pulling herself fully out of the hole, Tetha flailed on her stomach for a moment before the girl gave her a final shove, scooting her nose within a few inches of one of the memorial plaques. She hurriedly pulled her knees up under her and scrambled to sit, scooting away from the edge of the room. There was a thump as she steadied herself, and the trapdoor slammed shut, leaving her in darkness. The air was musty and cold, and it felt like a hand on the back of her neck. For a long moment, all she could do was focus on breathing.

Before she could speak, Tetha felt a hand find hers. Rough fingers tugged her forward, and the space seemed to change. It was less infinite now, less gaping, as she remembered she wasn't alone. Knees banging against the cold stone, Tetha crawled forward until she found her companion.

"Sorry," she whispered into the dark in front of her. "This place scares me a bit, I guess. Do you know how to get out of here?"

The girl pulled her up, guiding Tetha's arm back around her shoulder. Tetha could hear her breathing now, and the shift of her clothes and the sounds of her bag as it shifted.

"Hey, listen." They began walking forward together, more slowly than before. Tetha weighed her jumble of questions, picking through them carefully. "You know you aren't supposed to be here, right?"

The other girl stopped moving, and Tetha stumbled forward a bit. "I mean, it's all right, I just wanted to know."

Quiet. The hand at her waist disappeared.

"I mean I'm not supposed to be here either, I guess. So you don't have to—"

The flare of light from another match lit the room, and the girl held it between them as she studied Tetha. After a moment, she pulled back a bit, leaving Tetha to support her own weight as she reached her other hand forward.

There was a long, thin scar that curved up from the girl's jaw, pale and faded, clearly very old. Her lips were chapped, and the bottom one was bleeding slightly. There were a few streaks of dirt but her face was mostly clean, and her hair was shaved close to the scalp, leaving only heavy eyebrows to punctuate a curious expression. Tetha wasn't sure how to read anything of how her nose wrinkled, the upward pull of one lip, like an expression of disgust, or the focus of her eyes, unblinking.

The hand paused between them, then reached forward to brush at the scaling on Tetha's mask. Tetha flinched back briefly as the girl started to pull it off, and then they both stopped, frozen in place, while the match burned down. A quick exhale of breath, a wince of pain, and then darkness.

She had been here before. The realization hit her as the fear crawled back down her spine. It was odd that she hadn't realized it sooner—she'd gotten lost in the catacombs years and years ago when she'd tried to run away, having heard that there was a secret passage somewhere inside. Liffy had found her, curled up and crying, hours later. She'd made a cup of hot chocolate and wrapped Tetha up in a blanket, and hadn't even told her father. It was the first time that Tetha had known Liffy to keep anything from him. How could she have forgotten?

"You know," Tetha said into the empty space, "Liffy told me that they used to hold the festival up here, a long time ago. It was supposed to welcome everyone into the castle. That's why they light the fires up here every year at the end of it, not down below."

If the other girl had moved, Tetha hadn't heard it. "I guess it's okay that I don't know your name when you think about it," she said after a moment. "No one is supposed to be anyone today, you know?"

Veris had only explored the catacombs once, but she had a good enough sense of direction to lead both of them out. The layout was easy enough, it was stacks upon stacks of dead important people, one long hallway chaining together the circular rooms. It only took a few minutes to reach the door, which opened into a side passage of the main courtyard, and light. The edge of Veris' previous ventures. She stopped outside, looking over at the girl next to her.

She'd kept the mask on, as bedraggled as it was. Underneath, she looked sweaty and tired, but she was smiling as she caught Veris' gaze. Her grip eased now that they were outside, and she took some of her weight on her own feet.

It was later in the day than Veris had been hoping for. Not sunset just yet, but late enough that she felt a nagging fear as she looked around. The courtyard seemed empty for now, but that would only last so long. The procession would be making their way up eventually, and the lights would be up by dark. At that point it would be far too late for her.

"I can find my own way from here, I think."

The girl had let down her hair and was brushing it back as best she could into a more loosely tied back ponytail. Her voice sounded lighter now. Veris cocked an eyebrow, and saw her smile.

"You should put on your mask though. In case anyone else is around." Then she stopped, and smiled more broadly. "Wait, I have a better idea. Hold on."

The girl rotated very carefully away and began to untie her mask, bent over to ensure that Veris couldn't see her face. As it came loose, she turned it over in her hands, clucking disappointedly for a moment and then began to rip at all the excess decorations, tearing

161

off the lacy fabric of the fins, and the delicate, mostly bent spines that marched across the top. She let the pieces fall, looking over her shoulder only once as she worked.

Veris caught the hint of her smile, quirked against a cheek slightly flushed in the cold air. A dimple, and an eyebrow that looked as though it was supposed to be delicate but fought bravely and rather irritatingly against its confinement. And the same eyes as before, soft brown and searching. Then the girl turned quickly away, finishing the job and reaching one hand back, holding the now much less elaborate mask. The elegant green scales were untouched, and glimmered more brightly in the sun.

Carefully, Veris took the mask from her, and after a second, reached up to tie it around her own head. The fit was odd, not built for her more angular face, but it was no less comfortable than the one she'd been wearing before. Then she handed her own mask over to the waiting hand, fingers wiggling impatiently in the air.

Once the other girl had settled the new mask on her face, she turned around again, nibbling her lower lip.

"Listen," she said, taking a deep breath and puffing out her cheeks, then slowly letting it out, "I don't know what exactly you're doing here." She held up a hand as Veris tensed, continuing, "and I don't care, honestly. I mean, I'm curious, but I think that's okay. I just wish..." She stopped, looked down at her feet, then back at Veris. "Would you tell me, even if you could?"

For a long moment, Veris wondered if there was a way to say anything more than no. Then she reached into her pocket, brought out the tin of matches, and pressed it firmly into the other girl's hand. It was as good an answer as she knew how to give.

Tetha waited as long as she could stand after the other girl disappeared around the corner, counting to one hundred twice and reciting all the fragments of poetry she still remembered. Then she made her way upstairs. It would still be a few hours before she had to light the beacons on the wall, so she made her way to her room, as quickly as she could with the limp.

Liffy would ask about that later, and about the mask. Lying back on her bed, Tetha made a few feeble attempts to come up with a reasonable lie before deciding that she'd just face that conversation when it happened. Strange things were supposed to happen during the festival. You weren't supposed to try and make sense of it, or to press other people for the truth. Liffy would understand that.

Holding the wooden mask above her, Tetha examined the crudely carved wooden feathers. Next year, she'd ask for something more like this. The shiny metal and elaborate decoration made her stand out more than if she hadn't worn one at all. There were probably people who would recognize the mask as royal more quickly than they'd ever recognize her face. Wooden and plain was how it ought to be.

Until then, she'd wear this, and make sure the beacons were lit on time, as was her duty. Setting the mask down, she reached for the tin of matches, opening it carefully. There were only two left inside.

"A welcome to them all," Tetha told the crisp air, shutting the tin with a smile. "A welcome from us all. As we will share this light together, and know that we will walk together, and through the winter cold together, together we will stand."

The beacons at the castle gate burned to life just as the sun dipped below the horizon, matching their orange to the orange of the sky. Veris adjusted her bag, shifting the weight so that nothing would jostle together. Shading her eyes against the sunset, she watched the shape of her city fade into the evening. It didn't look quite so dull, from outside. The castle, at least, was beautiful, all alight as the rest of the world went dark.

She could buy her way anywhere now, she figured. Perhaps travel along the coast for a while, and then head for one of the mountain towns further inland. After that, she wasn't sure, but she'd figure something out.

The twin fires roared like a farewell.

Three Nerds and a Camera
Paige C. Wolfe

A year ago it took me 20 minutes to set up the camera. Now it took 5. I wanted so much to make sure every shot and every angle was perfect. My first video was a sketch idea I had in college, had workshopped in class and uploaded to YouTube without much of an idea of what else to do. Not too long ago, I watched that video again, and cringed the entire time. I was trying so hard to make something good that, to me at least, it lost all its charm.

Now, one hundred videos and four thousand subscribers later, setting up the camera, knowing how to get a good shot, and all the little tricks were memorized in my muscles. I was almost bored by it.

As I was setting up for a vlog, Dina sat perfectly still on our old, black cloth couch as I focused the camera. Then she started making faces and I laughed.

"Almost done," I said.

Video: Long Time No Talk

From playlist "Vlogs"

Dina and I sit close together on the vlog couch in our living room (Kennedy is still at work.) While we both make an effort to smile, an air of boredom seems to pull our bodies into the floor.

"Hello, my lovelies," I wave. "It's been a long time since I recorded a vlog. I generally use vlogs when there's a big update on the channel or there's something I want to discuss. And, well, there really hasn't been anything new since the last one. Obviously, I'm less inclined to make a vlog if there's nothing to talk about. As of right now, only Dina has a new thing going on." I indicate to Dina sitting next to me on the couch.

"I'm coming out with a new album next week," she launches right into it. "I'm doing something different for the music video, so I hope you all like it." Dina nods that she's done.

"Anyway, that's it. Short and sweet. I'm going to try to pick the vlogs back up because I miss talking to you all. Hopefully, we'll have more interesting things to talk about next time. Bye!"

Description:

There's not much to cover this go around, but I did miss talking to you all. Watch for Dina's new album next week.

Music by Dina: Day to Day

Comments:

lu ferby

Oooo I'm so excited for Dina's new album!

Lizy X

We missed you Audrey! But don't feel like you have to talk to us if there's nothing to say…

Pegasus Girl

Where's Kennedy?

Unknown Wizard4

Like this and your crush will ask you out!

Kennedy silently waved to me as she tiptoed out the front door to go to work. Dina was still sprawled on her bed from a long shift of bartending, and an early waking would make her cranky for the day. I waved back and went back to video editing as she softly closed the door behind her.

I played the raw footage for the next travel vlog, making cuts as I went. My phone vibrated in my pocket, and fishing it out, I saw it was my mom. I saved my progress and snuck outside before I answered.

"Hey, bun," said my mom. "Your father and I are going to visit Grandpa Jim in the nursing home for Thanksgiving. So if you're coming down then, that's the plan."

"That's okay, Kennedy said she wanted to do our own Thanksgiving here in the apartment, so I'm deciding to stay here. I'll be home for Christmas."

"Okay, then. Does she know how to make mashed potatoes like I do?"

"No, but I'm sure she'll make them if I ask," I said.

"Good. So, anything new with you?" Mom asked.

"Not really. Although, I met someone yesterday at the park while we were filming."

There was just the slightest pause. "Oh?" Mom said.

"Yeah, she was really cool. We're into the same shows and books. I got her number."

167

"That's nice," was all Mom said. No "what's her name?", "is she cute?", nothing. I sighed. I didn't know why I tried.

"Anyway, I need to get back to work," I said.

"All right, bun. I'll let you go. Love you."

"Love you too." And we hung up. I rubbed my eyes underneath my glasses while the familiar disappointment pulled at my stomach.

When I came out to my parents, they said all the right things. "We support you. We love you no matter what." But when I tried to talk about it, I'd watch their faces go blank and their responses to me switch to automatic. Dad was just awkward in general in a conversation about girl things and relationships. Mom, I could only guess, was just uncomfortable with my orientation. I didn't blame them any more than I did the time they were raised. It was just lonely to not be able to talk to anyone about it.

And then I met Dina and Kennedy. While they were both straight, they listened and at least tried to relate.

I stole back into the apartment, only to find that Dina was up and warming herself a cup of coffee. "Morning, sleeping beauty."

She gave me a look and I scurried back to my computer.

Video: Chicago Touristy Things, Part 4
From playlist "Roomdates"

As we stand on the train platform, I point the camera at Dina. Her face is barely visible around her cloud of hair, almost unaffected by the wind. "Where are we going, Dina?" I ask. She turns and looks at me with one of her expressions that say a thousand words. This time she's saying, "Seriously, sweetie?"

Kennedy pops into view with such an expression of enthusiasm you want to pinch her cheek. "We're going on an adventure!"

Cut to Dina and Kennedy stepping off the train and navigating the busy Chicago sidewalks. We get to Grant Park and I make a quick sweep of the landscape.

Kennedy's high-top Converse, then Dina's flats stand imitating the Agora statues. I zoom out to see Kennedy doing a really bad ballerina impression and then Dina doing Charlie's Angels.

Cut to the crowds around Cloud Gate. Every other person is taking a selfie, ourselves included. I hold the camera in front of me while Kennedy and Dina squeeze at my sides. Freeze on us smiling, freeze on us making silly faces, freeze on us being comically serious.

Then I follow the two of them down Lakefront Trail, trying to keep more of the water in shot than the traffic on Lake Shore Drive.

Dina and Kennedy find a bench and sit down. Here I get several shots of Dina's feet tapping a rhythm, Kennedy's fingers tracing patterns on her jeans, and both them talking (of their latest theories on *Outlander* but I took out the audio). They hold still while I take too many close-ups of their faces (you can tell by their smiles they're amusing me).

I just love Kennedy's profile. Her nose is adorable and small and slightly turned up. You can just imagine a tiny skier sliding down and flying into the air off the tip of her nose. Then you come to her feathery hair, which melds and fades into as many colors as a sunset.

And Dina's hair and eyes, they're so beautiful. You get lost in her hair following any wild curl up to her scalp. From far away her eyes look black, but zoom in and you see dark brown, yellow and even a little purple.

Finally, we take the train home where Dina lists off the hours she's working (audio taken out) and Kennedy nearly falls asleep standing up.

Description:

Grant Park, featuring the Agora statues, and Millennium Park featuring Cloud Gate (aka the Bean).

Music by Dina: Pretty Things

Comments:

Paisley Zz78

Beautiful! If I could go on a roomdate with you guys, I would die happy!

Sour Cabbage Patch

Where are the feet statues? I know they're in Chicago but I never know where.

Darwin K

Grant Park you'd know that if you looked in the description.

SalsaD88

Another fine example of how talented Audrey is. Gorgeous shots! Seamless editing! Nice...

NightRaven

Audrey, Kennedy and Dina would be the best roommates.

Snap, snap, snap.

We knew Kennedy had a bad workday when she had to relieve the stress by snapping her fingers.

"What's bothering you, snappy?" Dina asked her.

"Nothing. I mean, a client yelled at me today, but that's nothing new," Kennedy answered, distracted. Her fingers kept their offbeat rhythm as she spoke. Sometimes I could tune it out, sometimes I couldn't. The only thing that cured her of both stress and the snapping was cooking.

"So what's for dinner?" I asked, pointedly.

"I don't know," she said, still snapping. "That's what I'm trying to figure out."

"Aren't there chicken breasts in the fridge?" Dina prompted.

"That's for this weekend."

"There's pasta too," I said.

Suddenly the snapping stopped and Kennedy's eyes lit. "Alfredo!" And with that, she dashed into the kitchen.

171

Dina and I both breathed a sigh of relief.

We were in the middle of an *Outlander* episode when Dina spoke up, "Audrey, did that girl from the park ever text you back?"

"No, she didn't." I checked my phone one last time just to make sure. My one "How are you today?" text was three days old now and no response.

"Sorry, girl."

I shrugged. "I mean, it's disappointing but it's no big deal."

"You have us!" Kennedy said.

"Thanks. Love you guys too."

Kennedy's muffled voice barely registered through my noise cancellers as I plodded through the raw footage of her next cooking vlog.

"What?" I pulled one headphone off my ear.

"Who's turn is it to do the dishes?" she repeated.

I blinked, thinking of the pile of dishes in the sink, including the ones Kennedy dirtied to make dinner. "Dina's, I think."

The sounds of guitar strumming ceased. "I did them yesterday," Dina shouted from her room. "It's your turn, Kennedy."

"But I cooked!" she shouted back.

I rubbed my eyes from underneath my glasses. We had a rotation that we quickly learned didn't work, but none of us had the spare time or thought to come up with a new routine to keep up with the chores. "I'll do them," I finally volunteered. Taking off my headphones, I shut my computer and shuffled to the kitchen. The tense silence quickly dissipated when Kennedy offered to put the leftovers away.

"Thanks. It's okay though, I already know I'm staying up late tonight."

"Sorry," she fidgeted.

"Really, it's fine," I insisted as I rinsed dregs of alfredo sauce from our dinner plates. "If we're late uploading, then that's how it'll be."

"Okay." She spooned pasta into Tupperware dishes. Then Dina peered around the corner.

"I'll empty that load," she offered. "Sorry I shouted."

Video: Butterbeer
From playlist "Kennedy Kooks"

Kennedy stands in our tiny, clean kitchen, smiling so widely that her eyes almost crinkle closed.

"Hello, my lovelies. Today I'm going to be making butterbeer, and if you don't know what that is, it's a popular drink in *Harry Potter*. The recipe is in the description below if you want to try it at home."

"Is it like the one at Universal Studios?" I ask behind the camera.

"It's close, but mine's better," Kennedy says slyly, tucking a strand of her colorful hair behind her ear.

173

"First melt the butter." She drops a stick of butter in the saucepan on the burner. (Cooking videos always take longer than you might think. Kennedy has to tell me what she's going to do before she does it, so I can get the best shot.) I hold the camera on the melting butter while she swirls the pan.

"Then add everything except the milk." I follow as she measures out brown sugar, salt, cream, vanilla, rum extract, and cider vinegar, dumps them all into the pan, and whisks everything together.

"And this is where the magic happens," Kennedy murmurs as she reduces the heat. She sucks a drop of sauce off her finger and wipes it dry on her apron (the Kennedy Kooks apron a fan sent her and that she now wears in all of her videos). She gently whisks through the bubbling, thickening sauce.

"Do you think there will ever be an official *Harry Potter* cookbook?" I ask, holding the shot on Kennedy's face.

Kennedy shrugs. "I'm sure there's a good reason why there isn't. It sucks though 'cause *Outlander* has this really nice cookbook and no one's even heard of it. Whereas Harry Potter is a household name and there's nothing."

"Isn't there an unofficial cookbook?"

"Do not get that cookbook." Kennedy actually stops whisking and stares straight into the camera. "That cookbook exists just to make money for the publisher. Some of the recipes are untested, a lot of them are just traditional English dishes that you can get in every other cookbook in existence. And the ones that actually require imagination are just uncreative. I mean, what do you think of when you hear 'cauldron cakes'?"

She pauses and stares expectantly just behind the camera. "Oh, um, cauldron-shaped cakes. Maybe filled with something, like pudding."

"Right, so not pancakes! With lemon zest!"

You can hear Dina in the other room, almost going shrill with laughter.

Cut back to the saucepan where the bubbling sauce is thicker. "Finally, add the milk," Kennedy says, pouring it into the pan, "and heat until it starts to steam."

Little wisps of steam float through the overhead light as Kennedy turns off the heat. She pours the butterbeer into three mugs and tops them with whipped cream (that she whipped herself, of course).

"Try it. Audrey, try it," Kennedy insists as she holds her hand out for the camera. Two seconds of shaking film later and I'm holding my favorite blue mug with my faded high school graduation picture. I take a sip and come back with my nose covered in whipped cream and foggy glasses. Kennedy's not holding the camera quite straight.

"This is the third batch I've tried, so of course, it's delicious," I say, wiping my nose.

Dina appears behind me. "Yes, we're used to such luxuries." She disappears to get her mug.

175

Cut back to Kennedy in a straighter shot. "It's so easy to make, so if any of you try it, let me know how it goes. Keep cooking!"

Description:

Butterbeer! At home! Without park admission! Enjoy, my lovelies. Stay tuned for Adult's Butterbeer, and yes, it's alcoholic.

Recipe:

½ cup butter

1 cup brown sugar

1 cup cream

1 tsp salt

1 tsp vanilla

1 tsp rum extract

½ tsp cider vinegar

4 cups milk

Melt butter in a saucepan over medium heat. Add all of the ingredients except milk and whisk to combine. Reduce heat and simmer until thick. Add milk and heat until it starts to steam. Pour into 4 mugs. Add whipped cream if desired. Serve immediately.

All dairy products can be substituted with your favorite milk alternative. I recommend pureed soft tofu as a substitute for the cream.

Music by Dina: Snaps on a Pan (Funny story: Dina started playing her guitar to the beat of Kennedy's snapping one restless afternoon. I filmed it on my phone. I still have that video somewhere. I think Kennedy came up with lavender fudge that day and Dina wrote this song.)

Comments:

Lizy X

Omg that looks delicious!

Sour Cabbage Patch

Just made it! It's soooooo good. Its how I always imagined butterbeer would taste.

Average Gamer

Pretty good! Im not into the specks of butter that float on the top. Am I doing something wrong?

> **Luna Lavender**
>
> It might be the butter your using. Try using organic or natural butter instead of cheap butter.

Your Name

Evry one have an awesome day!

"What do you think?" Dina asked. She tried to sound casual, but I saw a nervous look in her eyes.

"It's definitely different from your usual videos," I said.

"So what, is it good or bad?" she pressed me.

"I like it," I finally decided. "I think it works."

"Okay," she breathed. "I need to tweak a few things, but it's going up tomorrow."

She slipped her headphones over her ears. What would the viewers think? Up until now, Dina's music videos were similar: for every note played, there was a splash of color as how her synesthesia saw it. A's were a deep purple, B's a clear yellow, C's a light red that was almost pink, and so on. Now she was taking a step away from that formula for something that was honestly really cool.

I remembered the first song she released on the internet. We had planned on doing a standard music video with live footage of her playing at Harvest St. Cantina, the bar where she worked. I had everything put together and ready to put online when Dina said to scrap the video and do something else. The last minute change only left time to put the song to her album cover and nothing else. The viewers were none the wiser.

Needless to say, I was mad. When I pressed her as to why she made me throw away days of work for something I put together in five minutes, she only gave me vague answers. It just didn't work for her, it wasn't true to her craft, she didn't like how she came out in the footage. Later she started playing with animations until she came out with a "synesthetic" video for her second album. I eventually pieced together a few things she had told me when we argued. She didn't want the internet seeing her play because anonymous commenters would focus less on the music and more on what she appeared to be: a chubby, half-African-American woman.

Never mind that she was extremely talented and feeling and her music reflected that.

I still had the old music video, and I watched it sometimes. One good thing was that Dina was right: her animations were more her style than my video was.

I returned to my computer where I was outlining for the next month's videos, and I got an idea. Maybe it was time for me to break my own mold and try something new.

Video: Bleed Me Dry

From playlist "Music By Dina"

(An electric guitar solo, pure and simple, supported by computer generated drums. There are no lyrics but you don't need them to know that she was angry when she wrote this song. She hits notes with more force than she usually does, and the song stays within a low, pessimistic tone from beginning to end. Sometimes I wonder where she stores so much emotion to be channeled in this way. Here and there you hear a few minor chords, which might suggest she's sad about something too. I ask sometimes when we're alone but she waves me away. I've come to accept that Dina doesn't express her feelings or thoughts through talking, especially if nothing would be solved by it. So she channels it all through her music. That may be her musical origin story, that she found comfort in music when her family wasn't helping.

All I know is that she wasn't angry at us. Or she would have said so. Thankfully.

As she rages through sixteenth notes, colors splotch over a white screen like paintballs on a canvas. All the notes have the same synesthetic colors, but instead of fading when the note fades, the color stays. As the song progresses, each note covers more and more of the screen until it becomes a multi-colored piece of splashy art. She's using it as the cover art for the new album.)

Description:

Written and produced by Dina.

Click to buy the album on Amazon.

Comments:

Dawn Joel

Not my favorite. I liked her old music better.

KaiserL

Damn! I just found my new work out song.

Storm Wind

I've always wanted to see Dina perform. DOes anyone know if shes putting on a concert?

Sofly

The videos cool but I found it distracting. I end up focusing on how the color was building up instead listening to the music. Plus it doesnt really fit with the style, its too bright.

Craze

Hey guys! I'm new on Youtube and just uploaded my first song. Check out my channel and subscribe. I'd appreciate your support.

Luna Lavender

Don't subscribe it's a fake account.

* * *

"How many bought the album already?" I asked Dina. She chewed on her lip as she scrolled through the comments on her new music video, with me peeking over her shoulder. It was the most dislikes she had gotten on a single video.

"Fewer than the last one, or at least within 24 hours of release." She kept scrolling. "So…I think the main thing is that the video doesn't work with the song."

"Or that it's simply different from your older ones," I added.

"That too," she nodded. "No one likes change, I guess." She was still chewing her lip.

"What's up?" I asked.

She shook her head. "It's fine. It's just less than encouraging when you try something different and no one appreciates it."

"I mean, the ratio of likes to dislikes is still pretty high," I offered.

"True."

"So what are you going to do now?"

She leaned back in her chair and breathed deeply. "I really don't want to do any more videos in the old style. I'm so bored of it."

I perked up at the mention of boredom.

"Plus, I'm sure everyone will learn to like it. So, I'll leave the video as it is. Or they can just buy my album. Either way, I get my money," she smirked.

"I don't."

"Yeah, sorry," she laughed.

"I'm also bored of the things I'm doing," I said.

"Oh, yeah?" Dina faced me. Kennedy also meandered into the room and sat cross-legged on Dina's bed with her recipe notebook and pencil.

"I think I'm tired of perfection," I mused. "It's obvious I know how to shoot vlogs and travel vlogs and cooking vlogs. And it's obvious I know how to make a clean, edited video. Now what else can I do?"

"So what, are you gonna be less perfect?" Kennedy asked.

"Essentially, yes. Actually, I want to make less cuts. I want to use more one shots of us, to show a little more of us. 'Cause I feel like I cut out a lot of who we are."

"Does that mean we need to start behaving?" Dina smirked again.

"No, still be yourselves."

"I was kidding," she returned.

"Anyway, Kennedy, I want to try that with the next cooking vlog. Is that okay with you?"

"Yeah, it's fine," she beamed.

"I also want to bring back the fiction skits," I continued. "I started outlining a script already. Can you guys brush up on your acting skills?"

Dina shrugged and Kennedy nodded enthusiastically.

"Speaking of the next cooking vlog," Kennedy said, "Dina, I want to pick your bartender brain. I tried both rum and scotch for the alcoholic butterbeer and they both work. Which would you say is better?"

"Hmm," Dina thought, "it depends on the effect you want. Can I try them first and give you my opinion?"

"Done deal!" she said.

"I'll try some too," I said.

For once, I could take an afternoon to relax. After making Dina and myself lunch, I curled up in an armchair to read a fantasy novel and Dina shut herself in her room. A couple of chapters in and Dina's chin was suddenly resting on my shoulder.

"What's up?" I asked.

"Can you do me a favor?" Dina was blushing, a rare sight. "Can you give me a copy of the very first music video?"

"You mean, the live one?"

"Yes."

"Sure." I resisted asking why.

Dina retreated to her room while I booted up my laptop. After I loaded the video onto a flash drive, I slipped it under her door.

A few more chapters later, Dina emerged to give back the flash drive. "Thanks," she said. She almost turned to go back but stopped. "Um, so I was going through emails from the subs. There are a lot more asking if I'm going to put on a concert."

183

"Well, that's nothing new. I've seen comments about it since the first album."

She shrugged. "The idea seems less daunting than it did before."

I shut my book.

"I don't know, though. 'Cause then I started researching venues and the good places are expensive and hard to book. It's a lot to think about."

"So why did you ask for the music video?" I asked.

Dina shrugged again. "I just wanted to see it."

We were silent for a long time. "Personally, I love seeing you play. I think everyone else would too."

She rolled her eyes. "Yeah, well, you're my best friend. You're supposed to say stuff like that."

"It's true," I shouted as she slipped back into her room and shut the door.

I stared at my computer screen. I had finished outlining each episode of the fiction skit and was ready to start writing. And I didn't know how to begin.

This was the first time I was writing in almost a year and there was a lot of rust to shake off. I had no idea if I even had a good idea. Would any of the fans even remember that I used to make fiction skits? Would it be so out of left field for them that they wouldn't like the change? I remembered the workshop of my first screenplay, and the ache from being told by ten people that something near and dear to my heart sucked.

I closed my eyes and breathed for a minute. Kennedy was experimenting in the kitchen and snapping her fingers, and Dina was practicing in her room with the door cracked open. I looked again at the blank document and typed the title. Then the first line. Then the first page. Then I had a rough draft of the first episode.

Video: Strawberry Peanut Butter Ice Cream
From playlist "Kennedy Kooks"
(Kennedy ended up just editing the description of her butterbeer video to, "To make Adult's Butterbeer, at the last step add a generous shot of dark rum per cup of milk." And that was it, no new video needed.)

Like always, the video starts with Kennedy waving to the camera in our tiny kitchen, wearing her hair in her cute nub of a ponytail and the Kennedy Kooks apron.

"Hello, my lovelies! Continuing on the Harry Potter theme, I will being making Harry's favorite flavor of ice cream, which is strawberry and peanut butter."

"For those of you who are reluctant to make this for yourself, which is admittedly kinda weird, it tastes like a peanut butter and jelly sandwich. What would you say, Audrey?"

"No, I think a PBJ is accurate," I answer.

"First you need to prepare the strawberry part."

(Kennedy and I changed up our normal routine. Instead of telling me and shooting a single step at a time, we arranged the kitchen equipment and ingredients so the whole section concerning strawberries could be done in one shot, me following with the camera as best I could without the opportunity for a second take.)

"Put your sliced strawberries in a bowl." She pushes a pile of strawberries from a wooden cutting board into a small, plastic mixing bowl. "Add the lemon juice." Without a cut in the footage, she pours the juice into the ¼-cup measuring cup and dumps it into the bowl. "And ⅓ cup of sugar." She measures out the sugar and adds it to the bowl. "Mix it." She grabs the wooden spoon placed perfectly next to the bowl and stirs for about 5 seconds, taps it on the side of bowl until enough of the dregs have dripped back into the bowl. "Puree with a handheld mixer or in a blender." She picks up the handheld mixer placed next to the bowl and begins blending the strawberries.

(Here I cut out some of the footage because who wants to see 2 minutes of strawberries slowly turning into a smoothie? Also, you could tell just from the tension in Kennedy's arms that she was feeling the pressure of finishing a drawn out take.)

"Set aside in the fridge." She takes the bowl and carries it off screen.

(In between this shot and the next, Kennedy told me the one-shot format felt awkward. She felt like she was taking too long to do something simple and wouldn't the viewers get bored? Her fingers were trembling. We reviewed the raw footage while Kennedy took some deep breaths to steady her nerves, and I told her I liked it and it didn't feel slow. I told her to go at her own pace and don't feel like she needed to rush. If I had to make cuts, I would make cuts.)

"Next we're going to make the ice cream part. Whisk 2 eggs in a bowl until fluffy." Kennedy cracks the eggs open over a bowl. She pauses for a second to pick a bit of shell that fell in with her fingers. A quick shot of her whisking so fast that it becomes a blur. "Gradually add ¾ cup of white sugar." Another quick shot of her whisking eggs while she slowly pours in sugar. The bowl begins to spin in place and my hand comes into frame to hold it still. "Oh, thank you, dearest."

"Mix in two cups of cream and a cup of milk and set aside." She measures out the milk and cream, adds them, and whisks.

"Next is the peanut butter part. Put a cup of the ice cream mixture into another bowl. Gradually whisk in the peanut butter. Audrey, can you be my bowl-holder again?" My hand appears and holds the side of the bowl. Kennedy whisks the cream while peanut butter falls in drop by drop. "In case you're wondering why the peanut butter looks weird, I'm using natural peanut butter because it mixes in the cream better."

"Why are you mixing in the peanut butter in the cup of cream rather than just adding it straight into the ice cream mixture?" I ask.

"What we're doing is loosening up the peanut butter so it mixes into the ice cream a little easier. You could definitely skip this step and try to add it into the ice cream, but I wouldn't recommend it. It's a lot of liquid and you could make a mess. You might miss whole chunks of peanut butter. This way is a lot more controlled."

By this time she was scraping in the last dregs of peanut butter with a rubber spatula. "And spatulas are your friend." (Also, have you seen Kennedy's forearms? You can just as easily tone up some muscle from whisking peanut butter as you can from lifting weights.) "Finally, gradually add the peanut butter back into the ice cream mixture." A quick shot of Kennedy pouring the peanut butter into the larger bowl of ice cream liquid.

"Freeze in an ice cream maker." She pours the ice cream into our well-used ice cream maker and turns it on. Cut to Kennedy holding the bowl of strawberry puree over the ice cream maker, speaking loudly over the noise. "When the ice cream is about two minutes from freezing—wait," she beckons to me, "Audrey, can you come look at it?"

The camera moves closer and peers into the bowl of churning soft-serve. "When the ice cream looks like that, slowly add in the strawberry puree." A stream of strawberry liquid dribbles into the ice cream maker, swirling into the nutty brown ice cream.

Cut to the ice cream maker turning off. "If you like soft serve, serve immediately. Otherwise, cover and freeze until firm."

Cut to Kennedy's smiling face. "So that's strawberry and peanut butter ice cream. The recipe is in the description below as well as some tips on how to freeze the ice cream if you don't have an ice cream maker. Let me know if you make it and how it turns out for you all. Keep cooking, my lovelies!"

Description:

Bring more of the Harry Potter universe into your kitchen. Enjoy Harry's favorite ice cream, strawberry and peanut butter. It's unusual but totally delicious.

Recipe:

1 pint fresh strawberries, hulled and sliced
⅓ cup + ¾ cup sugar
¼ cup lemon juice
2 eggs
2 cups heavy whipping cream
1 cup milk
½ cup creamy peanut butter

Mix strawberries, lemon juice, and ⅓ cup of sugar in a bowl. Cover and refrigerate for 1 hour. Puree and return to the refrigerator.

Whisk eggs until fluffy. Whisk in remaining ¾ cup of sugar, little at a time, and continue whisking until completely blended. Add cream and milk and whisk to blend.

Set 1 cup of cream mixture in another bowl. Whisk in peanut butter, a little at a time. Add peanut butter mixture back into cream mixture.

Freeze in an ice cream maker. Two minutes before it's ready, add strawberry puree and let ice cream maker run until blended. Cover and put in freezer until firm.

To the lovelies who don't have an ice cream maker: Don't add the cream and mix in the strawberry puree after mixing in the peanut butter. Freeze mixture in ice cube trays. Pop the frozen mixture out of the trays and put in a blender. Add cream and blend until smooth. Immediately transfer to ice cream container and freeze until firm.

If you don't have a blender, mix as directed and add strawberry puree after the peanut butter. Transfer to ice cream container and freeze for about 10 minutes. Remove from freezer and stir with a wooden spoon, breaking up any ice chunks that have formed. Return to freezer and repeat until all liquid is frozen, about 1 hour. I fully commend the lovelies who have the time and patience to use this method.

To my vegan/vegetarian lovelies: I'm still trying to find substitutes that work for ice cream. If you have one that works, leave a comment. Stay tuned and keep cooking!

Music by Dina: Snaps on a Pan

                        Comments:

Borderline Sane

I don't understand why recipes make you do half the things you do to make something. Which is why I liked it when she explained why you mix the peanut butter with a small part of the cream instead of just putting it directly in the bowl.

Izzi B

Just a lot of screen time of Kennedy whisking. Save yourself some time and skip the video and just get the recipe in the description.

Crackin Jack

I thought it was useful. I'm trying to be a better cook and it helped to see Kennedy's technique.

Izzi B

It's not hard to whisk. It's just stirring. With a whisk. Any idiot can do it.

Creative Cookie

I go to culinary school and let me just say that there's more to whisking than just stirring with a whisk. You have to use your wrist and forearms rather than your upper arms and shoulders to whisk because you'll get tired fast, which is what Kennedy is doing. You also have to keep up a high speed to stir in enough air to make the ice cream light, which is again what Kennedy is doing. It helps to see what she's doing because these things are not obvious to people who are not professional chefs.

Izzi B

You can also just use an electric mixer.

Cosmic Boom

Oh my god, not everyone can afford an electric mixer! I have to cook everything at home because I don't have the money to go out to dinner or get ice cream at the store because it's cheaper to make at home and I have every right to enjoy a treat every now and then. Every tip helps especially if it's gonna keep my arms from aching. So don't assume everyone else has money you privledged fuck!

Sweetie Pie Pea

Ewww she stuck her fingers in the eggs! I hope she washed her hands.

Unknown Wizard4

Geez calm down she's a pro chef of course she washed her hands. Also you are no more likely to get sick from someone sticking their fingers in ice cream than you are from touching a doorknob or shaking someone's hand. Think about that for minute the next time you complain about someone touching food you don't even eat.

"Can we go back to the original format?"

I looked up from my computer and Kennedy recoiled from her spot in the doorway. I was probably looking more exasperated than I had intended. Her cooking vlog with the new filming style was getting mixed reviews and more dislikes than Dina's new music video. The commenters were bickering about whisking and germs on your hands, of all things. The analytics from the channel showed that the subscriber count had come to a standstill in the last 24 hours, which compared to the slow, steady increase we'd had since we started the channel, could mean that the rate of those unsubscribing had increased. And if we lost viewers, then I wouldn't make my money to contribute to the living expenses. I was too engrossed in sorting out what to do about these bad signs to deal with anything from Kennedy or Dina yet, even if it was related to the channel.

"Can we discuss that later please?" I begged.

"Okay," she said in a small voice and retreated from my door.

My stomach sank and I immediately wanted to follow her out and apologize. One thing at a time, I told myself.

So my first attempt at changing the film style didn't go as well as I'd hoped. The more I thought about it, my decisions to leave in the moments of Kennedy whisking and picking out the eggshell had inadvertently caused the arguments about whisking and hand germs. Until now, we had been able to avoid dealing with commenters creating the kind of environment where stating your opinion risks retaliation rather than support and respectful debate. I had wanted the comments section to be a safe place, and now I was watching the threads get slowly nastier and nastier.

It was just a first attempt and I already knew I needed to cultivate the technique a little better, but the pushback was enough to make me think we should go back to the old style.

I didn't even want to think of what would happen if I released the first new fiction skit.

After a moment or two to breathe and collect my thoughts, I followed Kennedy to the living room where she was sitting on the couch with her laptop. She pulled out her earbuds when she saw me. "Sorry for cutting you short. I'm in the same place as Dina where it's difficult to get this much backlash when you simply wanted to try something new."

Kennedy shrugged. "It's fine."

"So you want to go back to the old filming routine?" I prompted.

"May I sit in on this conversation?" asked Dina's voice from behind me.

"Go for it," I agreed.

"It just felt awkward," Kennedy reiterated. "It was difficult to keep myself from wanting to rush through and I'm afraid I'm gonna make mistakes. And like you said, the way we were doing it left no room for retakes, and that makes me more nervous."

I nodded and thought for a second. The sinking feeling in my stomach didn't help. "I can agree that it's problematic and I especially don't want you to feel like you can't make mistakes. But what I liked about it is that you started talking more. Most of the viewers liked the part about the peanut butter."

"I guess. But the old style had a structure that made sense to me. I knew exactly what I had to do with each take. I knew when to start an action and I knew when to end it. With the new style, I just had to go and I didn't know if you were getting what you needed, and I couldn't ask because then that would ruin the take."

I sighed and shrugged. "Honestly, I'm not sure if I'm gonna continue with the new style anyway. We may be losing subscribers over it," I admitted, half-defeated.

"Well, I liked it," Dina said from her chair. I had almost forgotten she was there.

"You did?"

She nodded. "I can't put my finger on it. I think it felt more personal. Does that make sense?"

My brain came alive. "Yes, because that's more or less what I was going for." But now I was even less certain about what to do. Kennedy wanted to go back to the old style but Dina got it and appreciated it. And usually talking to them helps me make decisions.

"I need to sleep on this, but Kennedy," I turned to her, "if I decide to go with the new style, do you think we could work out a compromise, something that you're comfortable with and that gives me the footage I need?"

"Of course," she said. "I don't want you to feel like you have to go in a direction you don't want just for me."

"Don't worry about it, sweetie."

"Well, we support you either way," Dina offered. And Kennedy nodded her agreement.

Video: This Channel is Changing

From playlist "Vlogs"

The first glimpse of my face shows that I'm nervous. My eyes look unusually big and I can't seem to stop smoothing my already flat hair. I breathe then start speaking, "See, my lovelies? I told you I would pick the vlogs back up.

"I'm covering a serious topic today. When I started this channel, I wanted to make myself, Kennedy, and Dina a space to express ourselves. Dina with her music, Kennedy with her cooking, and me with filming. I never imagined it would become as successful as it is now, let alone a means to support myself financially. I mean, we're about to hit 5,000 subscribers, which absolutely blows my mind. My favorite thing is I love seeing what you all have to say or going to Tumblr and seeing the things you all have created. Just the other day I saw an awesome drawing of all of us posing by the Agora statues, and it just tickled me.

"Recently, I decided to try something new with how I edit and film. I used to make cuts to cut out long pauses or mistakes or something to make the whole video look clean. Then I realized that I was cutting out a lot of who we are. We're not perfect. We fight about chores. We make mistakes. I thought it would be so much more interesting if I put together videos that showed a little bit of that, to show we're human.

"You all may have noticed that's what I was trying to do with Kennedy's last cooking video, and a lot of you didn't like it. Which is fair, I admit there are a few kinks I need to work out. Kennedy told me that she felt awkward with the new style and we're going to be working together to figure something out that works for the both of us.

"Another thing that's changing is I am going to start doing fiction skits again. For those of you who were here from the very beginning, you would remember that's why I started this channel in the first place. I quit a job I hated and started making videos because it's something I absolutely love doing. But then I wasn't uploading enough videos to make much money or to build a viewer base. There was just too much time going into making one video. So Dina and Kennedy lent their talents to help produce more content more quickly, and that's how this channel became what it is now. The fiction sketches were sorta left forgotten, until now that is. I'm looking towards the first one coming out in the next month, and again, I'd love to hear what you all think.

"So that being said, I still want this channel to be a place for us to express ourselves. There will be more times when we try something new. Maybe it works and maybe it doesn't. Either way we are going to change and this channel is going to change because we all want to grow as artists. The universe knows I can make a clean vlog, so I'm going to try my hand at something else for a change. The same goes for Kennedy and Dina.

"The last thing I want to talk about is the comments section. I also want this channel to be a safe place for all of you to express yourselves and your opinions and get feedback. In the last two videos, there were some arguments that started because a few said they didn't like something another person said. Remember that everyone is entitled to their opinions, even if they're negative. We get more out of those comments than you might think. So please, my lovelies, let's be respectful of each other and allow everyone to have their say. And if you have something to say to them, maybe they're misunderstanding something, kindly let them know. We all learn something new everyday. If you see any hate comments, just ignore them. They want to get a rise out of someone, so if no one responds, they move on.

"Anyway, that's all I have for today. Please, let me know what you all think of these new developments, because I would certainly love to hear your opinions.

"Until then, stay lovely."

Description:

What the title said. We've all realized we're ready to make some changes.

Also please remember to be kind and respectful of each other.

Music by Dina: From Spring to Summer

Comments:

Officially Fake

I'll watch no matter what you do. You guys have felt like friends to me during some tough times and you still never fail to put a smile on my face.

not a hipster

Thanks for speaking so openly. We know you're not perfect and we never meant for you to feel otherwise.

Nimbus Tardis

Why would you leave in the mistakes? I honestly don't get it and why is this such a big deal?

John
It's like Audrey said, she wants to show that they're human and there's a way to show that in film editing.

HeWolf
I honestly didn't like Dina's last album or the last cooking video. The music was sloppy, video editing was sloppy and overall was just not as good as their old stuff.

mvemjsunp
You don't have to watch it if you don't like it. No one's making you.

Borderline Sane
You are all beautiful and deserve all the happy things. Have an awesome day!

I knocked on Dina's door. "It's me."

"C'min," Dina called.

I stepped in and sat on her bed. Dina was putting away her laundry. "I want to follow up on the concert thing."

"What about it?" she asked.

"Have you thought more about it?"

"A little."

"'Cause I was wondering if you could play live for the fiction skit," I said a little too quickly.

Dina was slow in putting away her jeans.

199

I was both prepared to push really hard for her to play as well as rewrite everything I had if she said no. "You don't have to decide now, but I know you'll be awesome and everyone will love you and even if—"

"I know. It does help knowing that there are some subs who want to see me play. So sure, I'll play for the skit."

"Oh. Okay, great."

Dina gave me a look. "You had a whole thing planned, didn't you?"

I shrugged and tried to look coy.

Video: Magical Craft, Episode 1

A shot of the L train screeching to a halt at the stop platform. The sky is still black with the faintest wisps of morning sun reaching over the horizon. Slowly Kennedy comes into view, sleep still in her eyes and tucking her face into the turned-up collar of her coat like a turtle (I'm not sure why I kept our real names for the skit. While I wrote the script, I kept thinking of some of the fan fiction I came across, and it made me giggle, so maybe it was a bit of a joke). The train doors open and Kennedy steps in, having no trouble finding a seat in a nearly empty car.

Cut to Dina sleeping on her stomach, mouth open, under a threadbare blanket. Brief shots of the clutter around her room, her guitar, her army boots, handwritten sheet music (with weird symbols over certain chords that most people know are not musical accents), a book half covered by a t-shirt so that the only part of the title you see is "Magic".

Next Kennedy hurries across a street to a little bakery, lights dimmed, "Closed" sign facing out. She fishes a key from her pocket and lets herself in.

From off screen as Kennedy sheds her coat, the shop owner says, "Oh, great. Could you start the turnovers? The milk delivery's running late so I need to go down the street and buy some." (Funny story: we may or may not have saved this bakery. We featured it in a video of our favorite haunts around Chicago, and then fans started to come by, hoping to see us and buying a muffin in the process. The owner pulled me aside and said the added business helped pull the bakery through a rough year, so he would say thank you with free pastries anytime we asked. Instead I asked for us to film here again, specifically to let Kennedy into the kitchen. He accepted on the condition we don't show his face.)

"You bet," she says breathlessly. The owner steps out. As the door swings shut, a gloved hand shoves a piece of paper in, stopping the latch from locking the door. From outside the shop window the silhouette of a hooded figure watches Kennedy put on her apron and hairnet and duck into the back to start mixing cherry turnovers.

Back in Dina's room, she suddenly bolts upright. She breathes, shaking off the fading memories of a nightmare. Turning on a lamp, she slips out of bed and grabs her guitar and an unfinished sheet of music. Dina plays the first few measures of a song, stops, then finds the book underneath the t-shirt. She holds the book up to see the title is "Magic in Music", and she opens to the page she needs, marks a symbol on the sheet music, and starts again.

Cut back to Kennedy stirring a simmering pot of cherry filling. She glances at the door, then pulls a small vial of brown liquid out of her pocket, and pours a couple of drops into the pot. She gives it a stir and leans over to smell the vapors. Kennedy grins and replaces the vial in her pocket.

The doorbell jingles and Kennedy shouts, "We're not open!" She steps out of the kitchen to see the hooded figure approaching the glass case of pastries. "Sorry, the door's supposed to be locked. Come back at 6."

The figure straightens and smiles at Kennedy (by the way, it's me. I started teaching Kennedy and Dina basics in filming.) "I heard this place has really good baked goods and I just couldn't wait."

Kennedy smiles back politely. "We're not open yet. I'm not even done baking, so."

"I also thought I would see the baking for myself," I continue, "see why everything's so good. You must use some magical ingredients."

Kennedy's smile fades, fear blooming in her eyes. There's a knowing look in mine.

Then the door opens and the shop owner enters with 2 gallons of milk. "Miss," he says, "we're not open yet. Please come back at 6."

I step away, leaving Kennedy rooted in the spot.

Returning to Dina, she pens in the last note, strums it through, then sets her guitar aside with a satisfied sigh. Cut back to Kennedy on the train tucking herself farther into her coat. The train stops, the doors open, Kennedy steps off, brushing past Dina as she steps on. Dina's hand steadies herself on a pole, then a gloved hand wraps its fingers just below hers. I stand with my back to Dina, studying her in my periphery.

The doors open and Dina quickly steps out with me not far behind, hood obscuring my face.

Meanwhile, Kennedy bursts into her own apartment, fumbling with her key as she locks the door. After dropping the blinds in all the windows, she collapses on the floor against the wall, breath shaky. She pulls the small vial out of her pocket and holds it up. The label reads, "Essence of Moondew: For feelings of comfort, contentment, and warmth." She returns it to her pocket and drops her head onto her knees, snapping her fingers to calm herself.

The sun starts to set as Dina readjusts her guitar case on her shoulders as she walks down the sidewalk (on my final watch through, I realized too late the continuity issue from the morning scene of her leaving the apartment to this scene. Choosing between delaying the upload to shoot an extra scene and releasing it as is, I decided to leave it be. People tend to not notice mistakes if you cruise through it with all the confidence of a perfect run.) At a traffic light she happens to glance back and see me watching her. She keeps walking and looks back again to still see me following her. Dina speeds up and slips into Harvest St. Cantina.

"You okay?" asks Dina's drummer, a lanky guy with a half sleeve.

"A girl was following me just now," she answers.

"Following you? Do you want me to call somebody?"

"No, that's okay. But could you walk me home after the show, just in case?"

"Sure thing. Let's set up," he indicates to the small platform stage.

Cut back to Kennedy peeking through her blinds and scanning the street in front of her apartment. Seeing nothing, she moves away to open her fridge, which contains nothing to make dinner. She dons her coat and sneaks out the front door, looking up and down the street before turning and walking down the sidewalk.

Sure enough, I appear behind her. Kennedy peers over her shoulder, lets out an involuntary squeal and starts walking faster. She turns a corner and finds a crowd of buzzed people outside a bar. I turn the corner, weave through the crowd, and emerge on the other side. Kennedy is gone.

Peering through the glass door of the bar, Kennedy watches me turn around and walk back in the other direction. She slips farther into the bar as the crowd cheers and claps for the duo on the stage.

"Thank you!" says Dina. "You're all amazing. We have one more for you before we pack up for the night. This is a new song and it's near and dear to my heart. Hope you all enjoy it!"

Dina takes a long moment to breathe out a shaky breath. She draws herself into a straighter, more confident stance and strikes the first chord. Kennedy and everyone in the bar go still, expressions vacant. She belts the first few lines, "Rise up against the crowd, stand up, the time is now!"

Suddenly invigorated, Kennedy and the rest of the bar start jumping and cheering in time with the drums. Dina plays the crowd with every rise and fall, casting her intricate spell with each note. Kennedy cheers like a fangirl. From the 5 minutes you've seen of her, you can guess this isn't normal.

The song ends and Kennedy blinks. She looks up at Dina and realizes exactly what just happened. The cheering dies down and Dina packs away her guitar while the drummer steps off the stage to collect their money. Kennedy takes the chance and approaches Dina. When their eyes meet, she says, "My name is Kennedy. I'm magical too."

A brief shot of Dina rooted in the spot, unable to say a word, then the title card flashes, "Tune in next week for episode 2!"

Description:
While the fates of two strangers intertwine, a mysterious hooded figure seems to know their secret... (Sorry for the cheesy I couldn't resist.)

Featuring Kennedy, Dina, and Audrey as themselves.

Stay tuned next week for episode 2.

A HUGE thank you to the owners of Davis Bakery and Harvest St. Cantina for allowing us to film at their businesses.

Music and soundtrack by Dina.

Sustenance by Kennedy.

Comments:

LifeWithoutStageDirections

OMG this looks amazing! Why isn't next week here yet?

Storm Wind

Wow... DIna is HOT!! Please put on a concert!

The Dork You Know

this looks so cool i;m excirted.

Zelda F

Audrey looks so creepy...Really good acting. Cant wait for next week.

Trash Bird

Where can we buy Dina's song? I found my new anthem.

Mt3t Ani

Your all beautiful

To Hold

Kristine Hauser

I.

The day Melia came of age, her mother set out a beautiful peach dress for her and smoothed the skirts with a satisfied precision. Melia let her mother pin her hair back with delicate clips, then selected a different gown, this one in silver. Mara, her younger sister, raised her eyebrows and looked at their mother, but nothing came of it.

Melia walked with her parents, her no less satisfied mother, to the palace.

Stepping into the Round, it was reassuring to feel as cold as metal. As they moved down the white stone steps and among the rows of wooden benches, Melia was surprised by the warmth. It was early yet, but the sky was cloudless and the heavy cloth coverings were pulled back, leaving the Round open to the world as it filled.

Melia's mother stopped to talk with some other women, but her father led her forward, to an empty bench close to the Council's table. The Councilors were scattered through the Round at the moment, mingling and laughing. Within ten feet of Melia stood the High Councilor, talking with a few of her children on the front bench. Melia had seen the High Councilor and her children before, of course, but never this close. Their backs to her, Melia saw their long, inky black hair. One of the daughters was leaning over to talk to her brothers, and Melia found herself admiring the curve of the Lady's neck.

She looked away. Her first time allowed to participate in the future of Jana, and she was staring at pretty necks.

The Round was nearly full—Melia didn't know if it was always this crowded, or if it was the clinging fears of bad news, of the Forst armies pressing closer to Janan borders. Pressed in with half the city's population, Melia felt anonymous. Her father sighed, but Melia sat up straighter as people settled onto the benches.

The Councilors found their way to their table, taking seats on the elevated dais and looking up and around at the gathered citizens.

The High Councilor remained standing, and began to greet the people. Melia's father leaned closer to her and whispered, "Listen to what she doesn't say—no mention of the Forst, no asking that people stay calm. She knows the Round. She's been the High Councilor for decades and she knows why people are here. They'll reassure us about the border around lunch, when there is more gossip in the back. It's more efficient."

She nodded. He continued to offer her such asides throughout the day, as her mother went back and forth between their seats and the back of the Round. Every once in a while, Melia looked over her shoulder to see her mother talking with someone. She was making deals and alliances of her own, though Melia didn't know what for.

Just before her father left to go fetch their lunch, the High Councilor and the Councilor General finished with one supplicant, and answered another worried about their border property. Melia's father winked at her as the Councilor General assured the gathered citizens that Jana's diplomats were hard at work making peace with the Forst King, and the army was prepared if that failed.

At this mention, her father frowned, but said nothing.

He slipped out after that, though he hesitated near the back of the Round as Melia watched. He dipped his head to speak to her mother, who put a hand on his arm.

Looking back to the dais, Melia was left alone to watch the Councilors. There was a sense of purpose and power on them, settling over their shoulders. The High Councilor at one point gestured for her oldest son to speak during a criminal hearing, and even from behind, Melia saw the same authority in him.

Her father returned, her mother behind him. They shared a pitcher of cool water and three lunches, packed by their cook's exacting hand.

The sun crawled over the Round, and Melia was uncomfortably warm as the Council began to wrap up in the afternoon.

There was some discussion, towards the very end of the day, about the new King of the Northern Run. The old King had been usurped by his wife and children, and now his oldest son had taken the throne. Melia's mother had said "good riddance," when the news had reached them at home. But the Councilors talked about the new need for relations with young King Won, with no way to know if he would keep his father's agreements. Melia saw, without her father's whispered point, why this had been left for last. It was kept far away from discussion of the other foreign threat, the Forst.

Jana had trouble on two borders. But between those points, justice had been done, decisions made for a stronger literacy program, and representatives of the farming communities outside the Citadel had confirmed that the crops were thriving under recent rainfall.

As the Council moved from topic to topic, Melia continued to watch, fascinated by their easy, capable power. She had learned careful accounting and how to create change from complaints on her Papa Rand's estate, when she'd lived there as a child. Her mother and now her father, her mother's second husband, had given her a sturdy formal education since. She had been taught to be useful. But this, this was purpose. The Councilors spoke and a country listened. They worked together and built Jana for their people.

Melia wanted that purpose.

II.

There was a hearing on marriage property rights a week later, held in the Round after the Councilor's dismissed their session. It was run by Yajun, the High Councilor's oldest son. Melia had been looking forward to it for days.

She had begun attending the Council sessions every morning, returning to her own work in the afternoons. The length and attendance of the sessions ebbed as the threat of the Forst did, though the Round was always more crowded when messengers were seen riding into the Citadel.

Her mother had been surprised, but pleased, by Melia's interest in the sessions. Her own work usually took her away from the Round, but Melia's father went with Melia most days.

He smiled when she told him she was staying for the hearing.

"Mara will want to hear everything over dinner, so take notes," he said, and kissed her on the forehead.

"You don't want to stay? I thought you'd be interested in this." She tried not to sound petulant in her surprise. He had given up his family's business to marry Melia's mother, who was above his station.

"I'm interested, but I don't mind how things have turned out." He was still grinning, still at ease. Melia remembered the arguments from before, between her mother and her papa, about the business Melia's mother had given up for his estate. "You and Mara will be better off if things change, though."

Melia couldn't imagine giving up her inheritance for marriage.

Her father left, and she thought about her papa, and her mother, and couldn't imagine it.

Wishing Mara could be there with her, Melia turned back to the meeting.

Yajun stood on the dais to begin the hearing but did not take a seat at the Councilor's table. She only recognized him from his wedding—glancing over the others she found she could not tell the younger two Lords from each other, and was only able to tell Lord Yamar from Lord Yidal because Yamar was Lady Yamira's twin. The six of them had stood with Yajun, and his wife Saranna stood to his other side.

Very few people had stayed in the Round, and as Melia looked about, she saw that they were mostly her own age.

Melia had worn her gold dress that day, ambition and excitement winning over her mother's choice of blue. She found that the low attendance did not deter her excitement, as she moved to sit close to the front.

They all rearranged themselves as Yajun smiled and greeted everyone. Then, settled in, he began to speak about marriage laws as they existed.

It was policy Melia already knew, but she listened intently. One of the younger two Lords yawned about five minutes in, but she noticed that all three Ladies were listening intently.

As Yajun finished speaking, his sister Yamira said, "All Councilors' spouses become Councilors in their own right, regardless of rank. We value that diversity of opinion and background, and the sacrifice of a Councilor's personal interests for their duty. But a marriage is not a Council. We shouldn't require a wife to sacrifice her living for her husband's."

"Or any spouse," Lady Ysolt interrupted. "Marriage is not always a blessing, and regardless, ending one shouldn't require restarting your entire livelihood."

"Still, we have to focus on policy," Yamira replied. She continued talking about how to amend property law, and Melia had to begin taking notes.

The yawning youngest son, she noticed, perked up considerably at one point when Yajun mentioned international marriages and treaties. "With the need for better relations with both the Forst and the Northern Run, protection for Janan citizens in marriage outside the country will probably come before the Council sooner than any need for reform within," he said, and Melia frowned.

She asked, without raising a hand or gaining permission, "Can't both be changed together? It's the same issue, in the end."

"There's no reason why not, but the Council will see one with more urgency," Ysolt answered. She caught Melia's eye, curiosity twitching in her eyebrows. Melia knew it was Ysolt she had admired that first day in the Round, and smiled.

"Not as their successors reach marrying age," Saranna said. "It doesn't affect this future Council, but the other Councilor's children, nieces, and nephews will bring it to their attention."

Melia noted all of this down. In the morning, she began to organize her notes and to make a list of what needed to be done to ensure she could keep her mother's business.

* * *

III.

A few days later, even as Melia was putting away her notes and lists at the end of the Council session, Lady Ysolt came up next to where she sat.

"Ysolt Lind," she said with a quick curtsy, even as Melia scrambled to her feet to make a proper one. The Lady's curtsy was a casual one and her introduction utterly pointless given her position, as though she and Melia were equals. Ysolt was beautiful, with a pointed face and clever dark eyes. She was smiling.

"It's an honor to make your acquaintance. I'm Melia Sorent," she answered. Melia found herself meeting the Lady's eye directly as she looked back, not sure where else to look. Ysolt was barely an inch taller than her.

"Pleasure to meet you, too. I wanted to invite you to the meeting in the palace tomorrow, after the session here ends. We're going to continue talking about property rights, and you seemed eager to do something. Yamira and I are hoping to get a proposal together by next month, and the more involved, the better. The palace is a more comfortable working environment for that than the Round." She grinned. "More intimate."

It was the way she said it—Melia laughed. She wouldn't have expected it from a Lady and future Councilor, but by the self-satisfaction on her face as well, Ysolt had meant to be funny. Melia remembered that Ysolt was only about a year older than her.

"I'll be there," Melia said, trying to remain dignified. She found it hard to stop smiling, though.

* * *

IV.

Work overwhelmed Melia in a few of the next weeks, but with it came satisfaction and an opening social circle. Ysolt was charming and funny, and Melia discovered she was blazing and sarcastic when faced with opposition. Her brothers and sister argued and spoke over each other, but didn't stand in her way when she pushed.

There was also Yarran, the youngest, and his advisor, Lyssa. She had a place among them and would certainly gain one of the two invitations to be on their Council when they succeeded the current one. She was whip-smart, and ambitious as Melia, and she wanted that invitation. Melia made a point to befriend her.

There were other two other young women who Melia grew used to seeing in the Round, named Chauna and Tani, who soon became friends as well.

But she found herself spending more time with Ysolt, going to meetings and hearings and talking in the back of the Round when they were both stretching their legs. Melia's mother approved in a distracted way—work had been catching up on her as well. She was almost always in her office, or in the back of the Round, gathering information and favors she didn't explain.

And so, for the first time, Melia enjoyed both the freedom of adulthood and of her own scheduling. Her father, of course, was thrilled by her political interests.

One day, near the height of summer, Melia told Yosim, the second youngest, that he was deliberately misinterpreting her point as they discussed the Forst. Her venom, usually more difficult to pull out, made Yamira laugh and Melia flush. But then she felt Ysolt's hand slide into hers.

When she looked over in surprise, Ysolt was grinning.

Melia didn't pull her hand away.

There had been nothing from her mother about a marriage, and all Melia's ambition and dreams seemed to point her to Ysolt. So when, a few days later, Ysolt pulled her around a corner laughing about a joke, Melia leaned in and kissed her.

It was light, it didn't feel binding or like a promise. Ysolt, still smiling, was kissing her back.

V.

Mara was draped over one of the more comfortable chairs in the library, reading poetry, as Melia wrote notes over one of Yamira's proposals. It was cloudy out and so quiet in the house that Melia could hear a branch hitting a window out in the hallway.

Melia heard the door open when their mother came home, heard her setting down bags and telling the maid to put something away.

"Did she go shopping?" Mara asked, swinging her legs to pull herself upright. She looked around for an exit. "Is there going to be a formal dinner or something?"

"No," Melia answered, still thinking about the proposal and the Round. Ysolt's hair falling out of its braids and against the back of her neck as they'd talked about the Northern Run with Yarran.

"Girls?" their mother called. "Are you up here?"

"In the library," Melia called back.

Their mother came in with a large, beautiful swath of furs over one arm. She gestured to Mara, who might otherwise have bolted, and set down what turned out to be two fur cloaks. She picked one up and swung it over Mara's shoulders.

As her mother smoothed the fur and adjusted the clasp, Melia began to feel a prickle of apprehension. "Mother, what is that for?"

"Don't worry, darling, I've bought one for you too."

"But what for?"

"You're going north! Lord Yarran is going to negotiate with the new King of the Northern Run, and in all likelihood, will be sealing it with a marriage to a Janan girl. You could be Queen!" She was still smoothing the fur over Mara's shoulders, pulling on the hem, eyes following her hands.

"The—The Northern Run? You want to send us to King Won?" Melia felt understanding slide out of her hands. She watched her mother, stupefied. "To *marry* him?"

"It's the chance of the century, my dear. Apparently he's very strapping."

Melia's stomach dropped. She heard footsteps and turned to see her father in the doorway. He didn't say anything.

217

Though nothing formal had been declared, Melia's mother had to have known about Melia's relationship with Ysolt. Melia knew, she *knew,* her mother would never jeopardize her chance to be a Councilor.

A throne was perhaps more tempting, but her mother's ambitions couldn't be that blinding. Could they?

She struggled for a moment to make sense of things, then realized she hadn't underestimated her mother's ambition, but her fears.

She had underestimated her parents' knowledge of the threat the Forst posed—had underestimated that threat itself, she thought with growing horror.

Melia opened her mouth to protest. She closed it again, standing stock still. Silent.

Mara caught her eye and shrugged.

"I've heard your friend Katrin is going as well," their mother was saying. Melia realized she hadn't been paying attention until this point. "And Lyssa Song and Chauna Aress."

"It'll be a long winter," their father added. His voice was lower than usual. "The roads to and from the Run's capital are impassable from the first snow until thaw, and with travel time, we won't see you for at least five months."

Melia turned back. She watched her mother watching Mara, fiddling with the cloak as though she couldn't stop. Melia wanted, again, to argue.

This was *her* future her mother was throwing away. *Her* plans, *her* relationship with Ysolt.

But it wasn't that simple. Melia and Mara had to follow where their parents sent them. It was their duty. They had been raised with their mother's dreams and ambitions on their shoulders.

This was *her* life her mother wanted to save.

"I don't think I can compete with Chauna or Katrin," she said. It felt like insolence, unforgiveable in the face of what her mother was offering her. "If they're going, they'll be planning the wedding on the way there."

Her mother forced a smile. She came to Melia and smoothed her hair away from her forehead. "You would be a good Queen, darling. And if not, Mara will need someone to look after her. What a wonderful chance for you two to see some of the world, some of northern Jana as well."

Her father hadn't come into the room. He stood behind them, like stone. Melia wanted to say—*something*—but leaned into her mother's hand. Her papa's estate, where he'd stayed since ending his marriage with her mother, was closer to the Forst border than the Citadel. Perhaps he had written something. Perhaps one of her mother's friends had heard something.

No matter how her mother knew, this was the most transparent goodbye Melia would get. The clearest order to live, and keep her sister alive.

She nodded and asked her mother to help her pack.

* * *

VI.

"You're going *where?*" Ysolt stilled in the door. She had come to Melia's house for her proposal notes, had stood in the doorway already grinning.

Melia had sent the maid away and didn't invite Ysolt in, feeling raw and uncertain. Her words had tumbled out on the sight of Ysolt's dear, open face. And behind her, a few rooms down the hall, Melia's mother was arranging her gowns for travel.

Perhaps she had blurted out *I'm going to the Northern Run with your brother,* because Melia couldn't bear to acknowledge the truth just now.

It didn't matter why—it was clear from Ysolt's expression now that Melia had gone about this all wrong.

"My mother is sending Mara and me to the Northern Run. As part of Yarran's party to negotiate the treaty with King Won." That was no better, but words slipped away from Melia's thoughts, just now. If she had been fanciful as Mara, things would have been spinning, or leeched of all color. As it was, she felt hollow.

"That treaty is—" Ysolt's face closed off in a second. "Oh."

For a moment, Melia thought she understood.

"You want a crown, then?" Ysolt said, blandly. "I see."

"I—What? No I don't."

"I thought you—I was wrong. Apologies." Ysolt was clearly working her way up to a fantastic rage. "Best of luck seducing King Won then."

The word was like a slap.

"I'm not going to seduce anyone. I didn't choose this; I have to go!"

"You could choose to say no!"

"My mother is sending me there, so I have to go," Melia said, punctuating every syllable. Why didn't Ysolt understand? "You would go, if the High Councilor sent you."

"I would never let myself be sent away, to chase some *throne,* when the Citadel needs me! When I have Jana, asking me to serve just as I am!"

"I don't want the throne—"

"Don't you? I thought you wanted your mother's business! Hells, I thought you wanted to be a Councilor! But I was wrong," Ysolt spat. "Or maybe you did, until you heard Yarran was going to go and trade someone off to a King."

Her cheeks had gone a splotchy red. Melia tried to organize her thoughts, to pull away from her mother, packing. Her mother sending her away from Jana, from the Council who needed her—

"I can't refuse her for this," Melia started and Ysolt stepped away, angry tears forming in her eyes.

"You could."

"I can't." Explanations came to her mind even as Melia and Ysolt stared at each other over the doorway. Excuses piled into her mouth but she couldn't say them. Couldn't say *She's asking me to save myself and I can't refuse her that.* Not over the doorway, where they would spill out into the world.

She needed Ysolt to understand, though.

"I can't," she said, and now she was crying too.

Ysolt left. It was not the dramatic exit of a Councilor. She didn't turn on her heel or have her family to engulf her, to block her from the world. But Melia knew it was a final and formal goodbye nonetheless.

She closed the door and went to her room. No one came to comfort her, but it was better that way. Melia took her silver dress from the pile her mother had pulled out to pack and put it back in the wardrobe.

VII.

In the fall, the Northern Run was beautiful, and its capital city more so. It held nothing on the Citadel, which had been carved from the white stone of the hills it sat on. But the heavy forests and foothills of the Northern Run had given its people more to work with. The city was built of wood and stone like a spoked wheel around the castle. The trees had not been cleared away for the buildings, but grew amongst them, providing shelter and grace to what would have otherwise been merely a functional cityscape.

Still, Melia could only imagine the barrenness when winter came.

They were welcomed into the palace by the Queen Dowager. Like her city, she was beautiful almost as an afterthought. It was not the first thing Melia would have said about her—she was struck first by her presence, her heavy features, and practical dress. This was a woman, Melia believed, who could overthrow a King.

"We're delighted to have you here," she said as she showed them into the main hall. Melia recognized her tone, carefully perfected to sound musical, inconspicuous. "My son, Won, has been attending to his advisors, and offers his—"

Before Melia could do more than register the excuse for what it was, a door opened, and a very large man came walking into the hall, reading something, not paying attention.

The Queen Dowager sighed. "Won, dear."

He started. He was what Melia had expected—broad shoulders and arms, unruly dark hair, and a sword at his side. He seemed to realize his mistake almost immediately, and straightened his posture to come over. He chanced an obvious glance to his mother for approval and she smiled.

Melia saw Yarran's eyebrows rise before he pulled them down with obvious effort. He was, as always, neatly groomed and his hair was pulled back into a low tail.

She could see importance, responsibility, on the King of the Northern Run, but on him Melia didn't find it attractive. She was sure someone in their group would, but already she ached to turn around and go home.

Instead, she turned to Mara and made sure her cloak was tied right before they were introduced.

* * *

VIII.

Time did not alter Melia's lack of attraction to the King, but ambition and habit propelled her through the first few weeks in the castle.

As the temperature dropped outside, the fires began to seem over-warm. But as the first snow roared over the Northern Run, Melia was glad for them. Winter came overnight, catching the landscape by surprise and sealing them off from the world.

Melia made a commendable effort to get to know the King, who was at least polite. Looking after Mara kept her hands busy, if not her thoughts.

Her heart was not in the Northern Run. Melia had been bored before, but the stretch of months ahead of her now was daunting. She felt pitiful, having come all this way for her parents' sake and now not making an effort at anything. Her work in the Citadel had been important sometimes, mundane others, but it had been *hers*.

She sat in the castle's small library, aching for home, when the Queen Dowager found her.

Melia straightened immediately, knowing that no matter how surprised the Queen looked, this was not a coincidence.

"Your Majesty," she curtsied.

"Hello, Lady Sorent," the Queen Dowager said with a small nod of her head.

"I'm no Lady," Melia said, throat tight and heart aching. "Miss is fine."

"My mistake, I'm sorry." The Queen Dowager smiled. Melia wondered where in this place she had learned such glorious false manners. She wondered what the Queen Dowager really wanted from her. "Have you been able to find anything to your liking here?" She gestured to the shelves around them.

"Yes, Your Majesty," Melia lied. "It's a good collection."

"I was speaking with Lord Yarran about all of you and he mentioned you had an interest in Janan marriage law."

"Yes, Your Majesty. Or at least, I was trying to change it."

The Queen Dowager laughed, and it was not so practiced and tinkling now, but came from her belly.

"There isn't much law in these books," she said, "But if you want, I could get you some copies of the Run's marriage law. You'll find it appalling."

Melia felt her eyebrows go up. "Your Majesty?"

"It has just occurred to me," the Queen Dowager said, in a voice that suggested she had thought about this quite a bit, "that some fresh eyes and fervor could do quite a bit to ensure that my son's Queen does not ever need to contemplate killing him to escape him."

It was an odd confession. The Queen Dowager's hands didn't look like they'd have blood on them. Her eyes, when they met Melia's, were frank.

Sparks lit in Melia's mind. "I would be thrilled, Your Majesty, and honored, to help you with that."

* * *

IX.

Her mother had wanted her to find a place for her and Mara here. So Melia went to work.

She amended the Northern Run's marriage laws until they were unrecognizable, and then brought them to the Queen Dowager.

"This is not my country," she told her. "I don't know if any of these changes are what you need, but clearly there needs to be change."

They spent days pouring over Melia's suggestions, over where she had made wrong assumptions or referenced Janan law as universal. As she worked, Melia felt the world open again. Change sat in her fingertips, in her words.

She spent months writing and revising.

Yarran sat by her, one night.

He wordlessly offered her a letter he had written to his family. It was a pointless exercise, since no mail or messenger could get through to Jana until the spring thaw. But as she read, she saw that he had included a note on her health and her efforts.

Looking up, Melia caught his eye.

"I know they'll be missing you."

"They won't," she said. She missed Ysolt terribly despite herself. She missed the simple ease of being with Ysolt, and wished Ysolt had been the one sent north. Yarran was young, younger even than Mara, and Melia suspected why the High Councilor had sent him. But she ached for Ysolt nonetheless.

"They will," Yarran insisted. "And you've done so much to help the Dowager Queen amend the marriage law, which will move our treaty match along."

"If anyone will marry the King," Melia said without thinking. She winced but then saw that Yarran was giving her an odd look.

"Haven't you noticed? Lyssa has her eye on him."

Melia frowned, mind recoiling from the idea instinctually. "Lyssa? Why? She'll be a Councilor if she returns to Jana."

Yarran crinkled his nose. "How should I know? She finds him attractive, apparently."

The face she made then must have been something, because Yarran laughed.

"There's no accounting for taste," he said. "You know, Ysolt will calm down, once she figures out you didn't really want the throne. Hells, even if she sees that face you just pulled."

Melia was not enjoying this conversation. She had resigned herself to the fact that Ysolt would never look at her again. There would be work waiting for her at home, and her parents, and the sun in the Round. But not Ysolt. Not any of Yarran's family.

She handed Yarran's letter back to him and tried not to hope.

X.

Melia didn't recognize the messenger, but she wished she did. He wore the crest of the Council, of Yarran's family, and he came barely days after spring began to show across the Northern Run.

Messages had been sent a week ago, at most, as soon as the roads were judged survivable. Melia thought, at first, that the messenger had been sent in a rush to announce that Lyssa or Yarran's family were going to finalize the match between Lyssa and the King, and the much-needed treaty that would come with it.

The messenger looked bedraggled enough. But as Melia sat in the throne room, watching him burst in even as the herald announced him, she knew that their letters could not have reached Jana yet. Even at his fastest, the messenger was too early to have been sent in response to theirs. Likely, the two had crossed in the middle.

She found herself rising to her feet.

Guards flanked the messenger, but his eyes went straight to Yarran, and he bowed.

Lyssa was on her feet as well, apprehension plain.

"What news?" Yarran said. Friendly and unconcerned.

Melia felt suspended, all her fears rushing over each other to clamor for her attention, even as she tried to push them down.

"Perhaps," she said, and her voice shook, but she pushed on, "we should hear the news outside of the throne room. We can retire to your sitting room, Lord Yarran."

Yarran looked at her, worried now that she had called him "Lord".

"I have a letter to be delivered only to you, my lord. In private, before anything else," the messenger said.

Melia caught Lyssa's eye, saw her own rising alarm mirrored.

"We'll receive the letter in the sitting room," Lyssa said, sweeping away from her chair, the movement so precise that it disguised her panic. Melia tried to move with the same assurance.

The guards, the three of them, and the messenger made their silent way to Yarran's rooms.

"Do you need anything to eat or drink?" Yarran asked, now more somber. He opened the door to his sitting room for Lyssa and gestured for Melia and the messenger to go through as well.

The messenger nodded.

Yarran's hands were shaking, too. Melia asked one of the guards to send someone for food, and dismissed the rest, then followed Yarran and the messenger through the door.

Without waiting, the messenger handed Yarran a thick bundle of folded papers, tied with string and sealed with a plain wax. But it was sealed with the crest of the Council.

They all watched as Yarran opened it.

They waited for several long, silent moments as he read. By the end of the first page, tears had begun to track down Yarran's face.

Numbly, Melia tried to figure out what had happened. Her imagination conjured up a dozen possibilities before she could even take in another, painful breath.

When he finished, Yarran flipped feverishly through all three pages, as if they would have changed. As if it were all a dream.

"What happened?" Lyssa demanded.

Yarran simply held out the letter and she snatched it away. Melia moved to lean over Lyssa's shoulder as she read.

Lyssa read at a remarkable pace, shuffling the pages as she did so that Melia felt the words flash before her, their meaning imprinting on her eyes even after the page had gone.

Yarran, hope you are safe and well. There is bad news—the Forst attacked the Citadel some weeks ago now—

The Council has been killed in its entirety—some citizens remain trapped, captive, but there is no way of knowing who—many died and many more have fled—

The messenger has what you need to prove your station as a Councilor, to find a way to bring the Northern Run to our side—it will be weeks before he can get through to you, but we are sending him now—

Have not heard from Yosim or Yamira—Saranna and Yidal barely escaped, but lost Yajun in the Citadel—Ysolt made her way here alone, on foot, arriving days after the rest of us—Yidal, Ysolt, Saranna and I are safe here, but we need you now—

Stay safe. If you can travel, we're where Mother always told us to go if this happened.

Many others escaped and made it here, and I have news of some of your group's families, below—there will be more by the time you get this—

Don't risk yourself to reach us—All our love, Yamar.

The pages stilled as both Lyssa and Melia saw the list of names below Yamar's signature. It was a list of the girls' names, Melia realized, her mind feeling distant, detached. She found hers.

Sorent, Melia, and Mara: Your stepfather is here, suffering from a broken wrist, but otherwise unharmed. He was in the Round when the Forst came, and sends his love. He asks you stay in the Northern Run until Jana is safe. Your mother was at home, and unfortunately there has been no word of her as of this letter being sent. We have word that your father has barred his estate against the invasion, and it is still secure. We sent him news that you remain safe in the Northern Run.

Someone had brought in a tray of food and Melia collapsed to her knees, to the side of Lyssa's chair, even as the messenger began to eat. He likely hadn't seen more than dried rations since he had left wherever the remains of Yarran's family had gone.

It was likely the High Tower, an old stronghold in the northern corner of Jana. It was where Melia would have gone, if she had had to decide. Closer to the Northern Run, well out of the Forst's first swath through the countryside.

Her mother, she thought, would have likely done exactly what her papa had done—barred herself at home. How much food had been in the larder? Would she have enough to eat, if no one broke into the house first?

Yarran was making noises that Melia could never have imagined from him. Deep, heaving cries, as he struggled to breathe through the onslaught of emotion. Lyssa sat stock still, but her face was swelling from tears. Melia, half-collapsed on the floor to the side of Lyssa's chair, saw that the messenger had stopped eating and was looking awkwardly at the ugly, thick rug underneath them all.

She noticed the pattern for the first time, a series of gaudy red and orange flowers, as a tight pain took hold of her torso. Like Yarran, she was having some trouble breathing and crying at the same time.

"We have to tell the others. And the King," Lyssa said. She had gone stiff and stony. Her eyes were still wet, her face still swollen.

"Tell the King," Melia managed, and her voice was not cold or even. She did not have a wall of stone inside herself to hide behind, not yet, and she continued to cry even as she pulled herself to her feet. She held her hand out for the letter, ignoring Yarran for now. "I'll gather the others and tell them."

News of the messenger had gotten around, and it was not hard to gather the other Janan women. They saw Melia's face and seemed to all freeze before her, preparing for the worst.

Armed with Yamar's list of names, Melia did her best. She saw, now that she had the presence of mind to read it all the way through, that notes had been added to some of their names, in a different hand from Yamar's. Last minute news being added, right before the letter was sealed. Melia recognized Ysolt's hand. She ran her thumb over one of the words and thought about Ysolt walking from the Citadel to the High Tower.

When she had finished reading, Mara came and clung to her. Melia stroked her sister's hair as they cried, as everyone cried, as Mara muttered, "They knew, they knew," over and over again.

XI.

Melia did what she could to turn herself as stony as Lyssa over the next few hours, as she forced the other women to eat, cleaned Mara's face, and took her sister out of the room.

Leading Mara by the hand, she found Yarran, the King, and the Queen Dowager in the middle of an argument in the throne room. Lyssa was nowhere to be seen, although as she watched them all, Melia saw the King's eyes sliding to a side door several times.

Yarran was holding himself together poorly, but was standing nonetheless. Lyssa would have excused herself at last, then.

King Won was trying to be reasonable, she noted. "Give us a few weeks, we can discuss a treaty and put together our forces—"

"I don't want to discuss anything! I need to go back!" Yarran might as well have stamped his foot.

"There's no—"

"We can negotiate the treaty now, then Yarran and I can take its terms to the Council," Melia interrupted. "Lyssa can stay here make sure it's fulfilled."

Mara's grip tightened on Melia's arm, but she didn't say anything.

"You have just lost an entire country. You are, none of you, in any state to discuss this," the Queen Dowager said.

"We are," Melia insisted, and felt as though the act of saying it made it so. She remembered her father, her father who was alive and who needed her, who was all alone in the High Tower. He had always chuffed her chin and told her she had a stubborn jaw.

She held Mara's hand and stared the King and the Queen Dowager down. The Queen Dowager conceded with a small nod.

"Now," Melia said. "The treaty."

XII.

Not quite five days later, Melia held Mara's face between her hands and said, "You stay *safe,* do you hear me? Mother and Father did this for us, and we have to do right by it."

Mara was sullen and tearful, but she nodded. They had argued about Melia going back, but by eldest's rights she had ultimately gotten her way.

Kissing Mara on the forehead, Melia let go of her and turned to her horse, to Yarran and the four guards who would take them home.

The journey was hard. Though the roads were passable, they were not comfortable, and there were no carriages this time. Yarran was all but broken, Melia discovered, and she wondered if she were any better. They sat together, shoulder to shoulder, around the campfires at night.

As they moved into Jana, Melia prepared herself for the worst, making herself comfortable with the weight of everything that had settled on her, with the emptiness of her hands as she looked around her country, now held hostage.

Little about the northern edges of Jana had changed. The Forst had come from the west and taken most of the southern country, had not yet turned towards the Northern Run. Still, Melia saw people preparing, shoring up homes that would be defensible and abandoning those that would not.

They reached the High Tower. The guards saw the crest of the Northern Run on them all and opened the gates before even recognizing Yarran's face.

When they did recognize Yarran, one of them was sent running into the palace.

Melia's legs were sore and she felt hollowed out. She fell out of her saddle onto the gravel courtyard. The gates were closed behind them, and someone shouted in a distance. The courtyard was bustling, soldiers walking in pairs and civilians carrying baskets of supplies. Yarran slid to the ground, just as stiff as Melia, but then seconds later was lurching forward.

Yidal barreled out of a door across the courtyard, moving around the milling soldiers and citizens with infinite care. It made Melia pause. She knew before, he would have expected the people before him to move out of his way.

Yarran collapsed into his brother's arms. Yidal nearly enveloped Yarran, tucking his brother's head under his chin. He had shaved his head, rough stubble just beginning to show. It was customary, for the grieving, and for a new Council when they took control of Jana.

Yarran began crying again, and Yidal was watching Melia. He nodded to her and said, "Thank you for coming back, and for bringing Yarran back to us."

"Of course."

There was more noise and Ysolt, Yamar and Saranna came into the courtyard together. Their heads had all been shaved. Yidal released Yarran and he ran to the others.

Melia's hesitation grew, watching them all. When she looked away, she saw her father being led out of the Tower by one of the guards.

She hesitated again, barely, before running to him and throwing her arms around his shoulders. He was not crying, but he held her like a vice.

"They said your wrist was—"

"It's healed now, I'm fine. Are you? And Mara? Is she all right?"

"She's fine, she's safe. I'm here," Melia told him, and had nothing else to say. She buried her face in his shoulder and found he was leaning on her, found she was holding herself steady to let him.

It was enough to let her pull away slightly, to turn to what was left of the Council.

She wondered if she looked as weary as Yarran, as Ysolt. Unlike her brothers, Ysolt seemed to be wearing a brave face as they all held each other, as they began talking about how to move forward. Melia wasn't sure why, and knew it wasn't her place to find out.

There would be so much to do. She had come here to work.

XIII.

Melia did not have time to write to Mara for the next three weeks. Her father took care of that, sending along a note assuring her that Melia arrived safely, and that they were together. That Mara's first duty was to stay safe and warm.

Her father spent long nights caring for the youngest children that had found themselves in the High Tower, giving parents precious hours of sleep. He usually fell asleep in their shared room as dawn broke, as Melia was throwing something on and heading to work.

She found that there was more to do than she could have ever wanted. Everyone in the High Tower was grieving. Yarran seemed to find comfort in it, in being surrounded by it. Melia, for her part, hacked her hair off to her ears and tried to ease the grief.

She organized lists of the living and the dead, talking to everyone in the High Tower. As she went on, people came to her with names, and she found them or she added them to the missing.

That was the worst list, the missing. Her mother's name was still on it.

She helped Yidal begin to keep track of the inventory they had and supplies that came in. He was itching for news from the

Northern Run, from small estates like Melia's papa's, from anyone willing to drive the Forst out. But while he waited, he watched the gates. He, Melia, and Yamar counted heads and mouths.

Ysolt and Yarran took all of this work and, to Melia's surprise, began to lead. Saranna was their enforcer and scribe, running information where it needed to go and making sure things were done. But it was Ysolt, with Yarran's patient knack for changing people's minds, who had the final word in the High Tower. There had been no official designation, no presentation in the Round, of course. But one day Saranna called Ysolt the High Councilor at breakfast and no one flinched.

After that meeting, though, Melia went and stood next to Ysolt. Put her shoulder to the other woman's and remained there for several moments. Ysolt had not broken down in front of her family since Melia had arrived. Hadn't confided in Melia, of course, but not in anyone else either. Melia didn't know what to do about that, so she just stood there and tried to remind Ysolt that she wasn't alone.

Melia, though she didn't mean to, did everything that the new Council could have needed as it shakily formed together. There had always been overlap, with so many of them to share the work, but now there were holes.

She found that ambition had less to do with her work than she had thought it would. She grew more comfortable with the weight of responsibility, but she didn't want to do it because it was comfortable. She did it because she could. Because Jana had not lost everything. Not yet.

Mara wrote back after receiving their father's letter, but her note arrived less than a week before the Northern Run's army did.

In the letter, Mara promised she would be safe, but Melia was not surprised when her sister was there, riding to the High Tower with King Won and the Queen-to-be Lyssa. All the Janan women had come back, Melia saw on second look. She smiled, and went to greet them.

XIV.

She had little part in the fighting that happened next. It was months long, and bloody. Yidal and Ysolt had raging arguments about it up until the moment that Jana's militia and the Northern Run's army managed to oust the Forst from Janan land.

Melia continued to look after the people in the High Tower, even as the population swelled, even as news of the Council's retaking of Jana spread.

It was good, distracting work. She did not dream or plan, like before, though Ysolt seemed more at ease with her than anyone else. They didn't talk about what had been said before Melia left, except once.

"I'm glad you were safe. I'm glad you weren't anywhere near the Citadel when they came." Ysolt kept her gaze on the papers in front of her, but her fists were clenched. Mere months ago, hair would have cascaded over her shoulders and hid some of her expression. But without it, Melia could see the furrows across Ysolt's face as she tried not to cry.

"I wish I hadn't gone. I knew my mother was sending us away," Melia admitted, and Ysolt didn't relax. "I just couldn't say it out loud, I was so afraid of it becoming real. But it did anyway, and I wasn't there to help."

"You're here now because you were safe then," Ysolt said. She shook her head, tension still apparent. "You shouldn't feel guilty about that. I—I thought about it, when I was walking here. I remembered that you and Yarran were safe." A pause. "I am glad you're here."

Not knowing what to do, Melia reached out a hand and put it on one of Ysolt's. It startled Ysolt enough that she looked up, met Melia's eye. Stopped trying to hide that she was crying, for just a moment. "I'm glad you're here, too."

I.

Melia went with the Council when they reclaimed the Citadel. She picked out a green dress in the morning without thinking. There was so much to do. It was a simple dress made for working and riding. But the color reminded her of spring.

There was no celebration, not yet, as they poured through the Citadel's gates. Even Yidal was somber and grave, despite his victory, as they moved through the city, up towards the palace.

Melia saw the residents who hadn't even left the Citadel gathering around them, joining the crowd that had come in through the gates.

As they walked up towards the Round, she looked and looked for her mother, but didn't see her.

She caught her father's eye, and saw a similar heartbreak. As the Council reached the Round, Melia moved to be by her father and Mara, but Ysolt caught her hand.

They paused, in the middle of everything. Ysolt said, low so no one could hear, "You're a Councilor, if you want it. We all agreed."

Her face was earnest, familiar, but everything was strange. They stood at the back of the Round, as they had many times before. Over Ysolt's shoulder, Melia could see that the Round had not been destroyed. Some wooden benches were toppled, but even at that moment people were righting them. The white stone pillars still stood, unmarked. The heavy cloths had been left pulled away to reveal the endless sky.

Then Yarran was at her side. "Come on!" he called. He was managing to smile.

Melia nodded.

At the edge of the Council's dais, though, she hesitated for one more moment, Ysolt's hand long since slipped out of hers. Yidal gave her a smile. Yamar was already calling for quiet. Ysolt had taken her mother's spot, standing behind her chair.

Melia stepped onto the dais, stepped behind a chair that could be her own, now, and cheered with the rest of the Round as Saranna announced them all as the new Council.

When it was time to step down, Yarran called out that they would open whatever food and drink stores remained in the palace. Melia felt a headache blooming. Ysolt came and took her hand again.

"Thank you," she said. "I'm sorry there was no warning, but—I wanted you to say yes so badly, that I was afraid to even ask. Hells, that doesn't make sense, but—thank you."

Melia looked at their joined hands. Looked up, at Ysolt's eyes on her. She hadn't dared to hope for any of this, to regain the Round and Jana and Ysolt's consideration.

"I've missed you," she said. It was the truest thing she could think of.

"I missed you too, and I'm sorry. I didn't try to understand why you left. But you came back." Ysolt smiled, tentative and unsure. "You—you can refuse to join the Council, if you want. I really do mean it."

Melia shook her head. "No. I want this, all of this." She took a long breath in, then let it out. "I didn't forget you. I didn't stop loving you. Even if you don't want—no matter what, this is what I want. I'll serve the Citadel, and all of Jana, and the Council."

Ysolt leaned in slowly, carefully, and seemed to take an age to finally kiss Melia. There was no room for misinterpretation. It was not going back to what they had had. It was a promise for the future.

They kissed, under the sun in the Round. Belatedly, Melia realized people were cheering, and felt herself flushing.

But Ysolt laughed, and kissed Melia again.

Acknowledgments

This book sprung into existence in a single afternoon, but it would never have made it this far without the love and dedication of everyone involved. There are too many of you to name or count, but this book is yours as much as mine.

Thank you to everyone who encouraged me, often in the smallest ways, for pages and pages. You have all been wonderful, asking after the book over and over again until I could finally tell you how to get it.

Thank you to my authors, for blessing me with your enthusiasm and talent. You were the driving force behind this anthology and I hope it does you proud.

Special thanks to my editing team—Chloe, Emma, and Paige. Your perspectives and insights were priceless over the months it took to turn my too-long premise into seven wonderful stories.

Eternal gratitude to Peter and Jane Kampion, for making everything seem possible. To Kaitlyn, for giving me the ambition to understand that most things are.

And finally, to Paul and Angie Hauser. Thank you for giving me a love of reading and a taste for drama. For giving me a lifetime of courage and honesty and laughter. You have all my love, enough to fill another few dozen books.

About the Authors

Kristine Hauser (*To Hold,* managing editor) is the founder of Spring Breeze Books, which seeks to create and publish diverse literature. She can be found at queenofthiuria.tumblr.com, or on Twitter as @k_hause. She lives in Chicago.

K.R. Kampion (*Queen of the Guardhouse,* marketing) graduated with a B.A. and Honors in English and Creative Writing from the University of Iowa. Education in hand, she's currently working on the steampunk western *Reconstruction* series. The first two books are available for free at jukepop.com. She can be found during her spare moments reading, watching too much TV, weeping over her D&D characters, and working out.

Ashlee Kilpatrick (*Ungodly Hour*) is a freelance writer from Fayetteville, North Carolina and has a bachelor's degree in Social Work from Fayetteville University. She enjoys writing young adult, science fiction, and adventure stories.

Chloe Leach (*Empty Spaces,* editor) graduated from the University of Iowa with a B.A. in English and a focus on creative writing. She primarily writes young adult fantasy and science fiction, and is currently working to complete her first full-length novel.

Stephanie Smith (*Glamor and Thread*) graduated from the University of Iowa with a B.A. in English. She currently lives in Texas and complains regularly about the weather.

Emma Van Dyke (*Magnifikat*, editor, cover art & design) graduated from University of Iowa with a B.A. in English. She can play two chords on the banjo.

Paige C. Wolfe (*Three Nerds and a Camera*, editor) started writing when she was 11. She attended University of Iowa where she met most of the authors of this anthology, all who nudged her writing in the right direction. In her rare moments of free time, she cooks, plays D&D, and watches too much YouTube.

Made in the USA
San Bernardino, CA
15 June 2017